Beware of the Cat

Beware
of the Cat

Stories of Feline Fantasy and Horror

Edited by Michel Parry

Taplinger Publishing Company / New York

ACKNOWLEDGMENTS

The editor wishes to thank the following authors, their executors, trustees, or agents, and the publishers for permission to include copyright material in this book:

"Beware the Cat" by Gulielmus Baldwin. Copyright © 1972 by Michel Parry.

"The Grey Cat" by Barry Pain. Copyright 1901 by Barry Pain. Reprinted from *Stories in the Dark* by permission of the Richard Press.

"The King of Cats" by Stephen Vincent Benét. Copyright 1938 by Stephen Vincent Benét. Copyright renewed 1963 by Thomas C. Benét, Stephanie B. Mahin and Rachel Benét Lewis. Reprinted from *The Selected Works of Stephen Vincent Benét* by permission of Brandt and Brandt and the publishers, Holt, Rinehart & Winston, Inc.

"The Vampire Cat." Copyright © 1972 by Michel Parry.

"The Cat Man" by Byron Liggett. Copyright © 1960 by Scholastic Magazines, Inc. Reprinted from *Story* by permission of Scholastic Magazines, Inc.

"Ancient Sorceries" by Algernon Blackwood. Copyright 1908 by Algernon Blackwood. Reprinted from *Strange Stories* by permission of The Public Trustee and A. P. Watt & Son.

"Tobermory" by Saki (H. H. Munro). Reprinted from *The Short Stories of Saki* by permission of The Viking Press.

"Fluffy" by Theodore Sturgeon. Copyright 1947 by Theodore Sturgeon. Reprinted from *E Pluribus Unicorn* by permission of the author's agent, E. J. Carnell.

"Cat and Mouse" by Ramsay Campbell. Copyright © 1972 by Ramsey Campbell. Published by arrangement with the author.

"The Cats of Ulthar" by H. P. Lovecraft. Copyright © 1965 by August Derleth. Reprinted from *Dagon* by permission of the Scott Meredith Literary Agency.

"The Child Watcher" by Ernest Harrison. Copyright © 1958 by Davis Publications, Inc. Reprinted from *Ellery Queen's Mystery Magazine* by permission of the author and Davis Publications, Inc.

Every effort has been made to trace the copyright owners of these stories. The editor offers his apologies in the event of any necessary acknowledgment being accidentally omitted.

DRAWINGS BY NANCY LOU GAHAN

CONTENTS

He said unto her, He believed she was a Witch. Whereat she being dissatisfied said, That some she-Devil would shortly fetch him away! Which words were heard by others, as well as himself. The Night following, as he lay in his Bed, there came in at the Window, the likeness of a Cat, which flew upon him, took fast hold of his Throat, lay on him a considerable while, and almost killed him. At length he remembered what Susanna Martin had threat'ned the Day before; and with much striving he cried out, Avoid, thou She-Devil! In the name of God the Father, the Son, and the Holy Ghost, Avoid! Whereupon it left him, leap'd on the Floor, and flew out at the Window.

Cotton Mather, *The Wonders of the Invisible World*

INTRODUCTION

A Cat, with its phosphorescent eyes that shine like lanterns, and sparks flashing from its back, moves fearlessly through the darkness, where it meets wandering ghosts, witches, alchemists, necromancers, grave-robbers, lovers, thieves, murderers, grey-cloaked patrols, and all the obscene larvae that only emerge at night.

—Théophile Gautier

"THRICE THE BRINDED cat hath mew'd" is the signal in *Macbeth* for the Three Witches to commence their rites and incantations—and rightly so for, by common consent, no creature has been so closely associated with witchcraft and the Powers of Darkness as the mysterious and night-erring Cat. Rare is the picture showing scenes of medieval sorcery where a Cat, no doubt nourished on blood from some supernumerary nipple, is not somewhere lurking and, in modern films and cartoons, a black Cat is as necessary a tool of a witch's trade as the familiar broomstick.

Very early on was the Cat chosen as a symbol of evil, or, at least, the Unknown, and there are few cultures which do not possess a legend in which the local hero fought and overcame some Monster Cat in the days when the Earth was young. King Arthur, for example, is said to have slain such a creature.

It is not difficult to imagine how the Cat's unenviable reputation came into being, for it is surely the most enigmatic of animals. It can be fierce and lustful or else serenely meditative. One moment it is part of the family scene, an imperious sophisticate lounging before the fire; the next it is transformed into a raging beast, a spitting fury of fang and claw, uttering near-human wails that pierce the night and freeze the blood. Moreover, quite apart from its appearance—the unearthly eyes, the bristling, sparking fur, the claws, the needle-teeth; all the prerequisites, in fact, one demands of a good demon—the cat is nocturnal, alone prowling the passages of night when all the rest of God's creatures are expected to sleep. Such rebellious independence was bound to attract attention and, in consequence, the Cat has been either worshipped as a god or vilified and hunted as an emissary of the Devil—if not actually accused of being Satan himself!

With such mystique surrounding it, it is hardly surprising that the Cat endeared itself to poets and writers celebrating the darker human instincts through images of the weird and fantastic. H. P. Lovecraft wrote that the Cat appeals "to the deepest fonts of imagination and cosmic perception in the human mind" and the truth of this is attested by the devotion to Cats shown by such writers as Swinburne, Poe, Baudelaire and Gautier. And, apart from Lovecraft himself, we may count August Derleth and Fritz Leiber as being among the modern masters of the macabre who are also cat-lovers.

Most writers of horror stories have written a tale or two about Cats and in this collection I have brought together some of the best —though not *all* the best. That would require a volume at least twice this size. Among the more obvious omissions are Edgar Allan Poe's *The Black Cat* and *The Squaw* by Bram Stoker. Fine as these two stories are, as they have appeared in so many recent anthologies, it is surely preferable to allow them a rest and give an airing to lesser known but no less worthwhile tales like *The Black Cat* by William Wintle and *The Grey Cat* by Barry Pain.

There are fourteen Cats lurking in these pages, waiting to pounce upon the unwary reader, and they are alike only in one respect—all are frightening. Even the Devil would hesitate to take any of *them* as a pet!

What makes these Cats so murderous? As anyone who has seen one playing with a mouse will know, Cats are exceedingly cruel— at least by conventional human standards. But cruelty alone is not the answer. There is a deeper motivation that must surely be *revenge*. For, strange as it may sound in these days of luxury cat-food, Man has treated the Cat abominably. Take, for example, the quaint old custom of whipping, beating or burning some terrified Cat to death to celebrate a good harvest or other festive occasion. Or the common practice of walling a cat up alive in the foundations of a house to bring good luck to future occupants. And lest we should think such deeds were confined to barbaric Satan-worshippers, we would do well to remember that Westminster Abbey stands upon the remains of just such an unfortunate Cat. Then there was the *Taigheirm*, the ghastly ritual in which the God-fearing and respected citizens of Scotland roasted black Cats alive on a spit, one after the other, for four consecutive days and nights in order to gain the gift of second sight. The eyes, whiskers, tails and entrails of a Cat have all been credited, at one time or another, with the power of healing or possessing some other magical property, and countless thousands of Cats suffered as a result. Once, during a supposed witchcraft epidemic, the belief grew that one could only be saved from bewitchment by boiling a black Cat alive and keeping one of its bones as a charm. For years, not a single black Cat was to be found alive in the region. And this was not in some backward part of Europe during the Middle Ages but in the American state of Pennsylvania in 1929!

It is said that if you take one of a Cat's nine lives, it spends the next eight haunting you to your doom. As can be seen from the above, the Cats certainly have a lot of haunting to do.

So Beware! And, tonight, after you have read some of these stories, don't forget to put the Cat out.

Before it puts *you* out.

MICHEL PARRY

BEWARE THE CAT

by Gulielmus Baldwin

WHEN I FIRST *embarked on* Beware of the Cat *I was rather pleased with what I thought was a clever and original choice of title. Imagine then my disappointment when I found that I had been anticipated by four hundred years! For it was in 1551 that Gulielmus (or William) Baldwin wrote and published a rare and curious volume entitled* Beware the Cat.

The first half of this strange work uses the conventional contemporary device of assembling a party of travellers and letting them swap weird stories—in this instance stories about Cats. In the second half the narrator, by means of spells and a grisly magic cake,* is able to understand the language of Cats and so eavesdrop on some fantastic conversations among the local felines. The book ends, appropriately, with an exhortation for the reader to take more care in what he says in front of the household tabby and, above all, to Beware the Cat.

Little is known about Baldwin except that he started his career as servant to a publisher and rose to become an influential editor and printer. He is best remembered as editor and contributor to A Mirror For Magistrates (1559), *a lengthy Boccaccio-inspired collection of tragedies and misdeeds among the nobility.*

No copy of the first edition of Beware the Cat *is known to exist today but, fortunately, a reprinted edition of 1570 has survived. The following extract is representative of the first half of the work. In order to make it more readable today I have made slight changes in spelling and punctuation without, I hope, losing the fine flavour of the original.*

* See p. 189.

Once I was in Ireland in the time that Macmorro and all the rest of the wild lords were the King's enemies, during which time mortal strife was between the Fitzhonies and the Prior and Covent of the Abbey of Tinthern, who counted themselves the King's friends and subjects and whose neighbour was Cayn Macort, a wilde Irish man, then the King's enemy and one which daily made inrodes into the county of Washford and burned such towns and carried away all such cattell as he might come by. By means whereof all the country from Climin to Roffe became a wilde wilderness and is scarce recovered unto this day. In this time, I say, as I was on a night at Corberry with one of the Fitzburies' churles, we fell in talk as we have done now, of strange adventures, and of cats; and there, among other things, the churl (for so they call all farmers and husbands-men) told me as ye shall hear.

"There was (not seven years past) a kern of John Butlers dwelling in the county of Bantry called Patrick Apore, who minding to make a prey in the night upon Cager Makent, his master's enemy, got him with his boy, for so they call their horse keepers, even if they be ever so old knaves, into his country, and in the night time entered into a town of two houses, and broke in and slew the people, and then took such cattle as they found, which was a cow and a sheep and departed therewith homewards; but fearing they should be pursued, the cur dogs making such a shrill barking, he got into a church, thinking to lurk there till midnight was past, for he was sure that no one would suspect or seek him, for the wild Irish men have had churches in such reverence (till our men taught them the contrary) that they never would, nor durst, rob aught hence or hurt any man that took the church yard for sanctuary, not even if he had killed his father. And while the kern was in the church, he thought it best to dine for he had eaten little that day, wherefore he made his boy go gather sticks and strike fire with his flints and make a fire in the church, and he killed the sheep and, after the Irish fashion, layed it thereupon and roasted it.

"But when it was ready, and he thought to eat it, there came in a cat who sat herself by him and said in Irish, *Shane foel*, which is, 'Give me some meat'. He, mazed at this, gave her the quarter that was in his hand, which immediately she did eat up, and asked for more till she had consumed all the sheep. And, like a cormorant not satisfied therewith, she asked still for more, whereupon they supposed it were the Devil himself and therefore, thinking it wisdom to please him, killed the cow which they had stolen, and when they had flayed it, gave the cat a quarter which she immediately devoured. Then they gave her two other quarters and, in the meanwhile, after their native fashion, they did cut a piece of the hide and prickt it upon four stakes which they set about the fire, and therein they placed a piece of the cow for themselves, and with the rest of the hide they made each of them bags to wear about their feet, like brogues, both to keep their feet from hurt all the next day, and also to serve for meat the next night, by boyling them upon coals, if they could get none other.

"By this time, the cat had eaten three quarters and called for more, wherefore they gave that which was a-seething by the fire and doubting lest when she had eaten that she would eat them too, because they had no more for her, they got themselves out of the church, and the kern took his horse and away he rode as fast as he could hie. When he was a mile or two from the church the moon began to shine and the boy espied the cat upon his master's horse behind him, whereupon the kern took his dart and, turning his face towards her, flung it and struck her through with it. But immediately there came such a hoarde of cats that after a long fight with them his boy was killed and eaten up and he himself (as good and swift as his horse was) had much to do to escape.

"When he was come home, all weary and hungry, and had put off his harness, which was a corset of mail and like a shirt, and his helmet, which was gilt leather and crested with other skin, he sat himself down by his wife and told her his adventure—upon hearing which the kitten which his wife kept, scarce half a year old, started up and said, 'Hast thou killed Grimallykin?' and straightway plunged in his face and with her teeth took him by the throat and, ere she could be plucked away, she had strangled him."

THE GREY CAT

by Barry Pain

BARRY PAIN (1864–1928) *gave up a promising job as an army coach for the uncertainties of a journalist's life and became a successful writer, the author of several novels and many collections of excellent short stories. Among his creations was* Constantine Dix, *a likeable criminal rogue whose exploits once rivalled those of* Raffles *in popularity. Although he is chiefly remembered as a satirist, specializing in perceptive jibes at dwellers in the suburbs and East End of London, Pain was passionately interested in the Occult—an interest which* The Grey Cat *vividly reflects.*

I heard this story from Archdeacon M——. I should imagine that it would not be very difficult, by trimming it a little and altering the facts here and there, to make it capable of some simple explanation; but I have preferred to tell it as it was told to me.

After all, there is some explanation possible, even if there is not one definite and simple explanation clearly indicated. It must rest with the reader whether he will prefer to believe that some of the so-called uncivilized races may possess occult powers transcending anything of which the so-called civilized are capable, or whether he will consider that a series of coincidences is sufficient to account for the extraordinary incidents which, in a plain brief way, I am about to relate. It does not seem to me essential to state which view I hold myself, or if I hold neither, and have reasons for not stating a third possible explanation.

I must add a word or two with regard to Archdeacon M——. At the time of this story he was in his fiftieth year. He was a fine scholar, a man of considerable learning. His religious views were remarkably broad; his enemies said remarkably thin. In his younger days he had been something of an athlete, but owing to age, sedentary habits, and some amount of self-indulgence, he had grown stout, and no longer took exercise in any form. He had no nervous trouble of any kind. His death, from heart disease, took place about three years ago. He told me the story twice, at my request; there was an interval of about six weeks between the two narrations; some of the details were elicited by questions of my own. With this preliminary note, we may proceed to the story.

* * *

In January 1881, Archdeacon M——, who was a great admirer of Tennyson's poetry, came up to London for a few days, chiefly in order to witness the performance of "The Cup", at the Lyceum. He was not present on the first night (Monday, 3 January), but on a later night in the same week. At that time, of course, the poet had not received his peerage, nor the actor his knighthood.

On leaving the theatre, less satisfied with the play than with the magnificence of the setting, the Archdeacon found some slight difficulty in getting a cab. He walked a little way down the Strand to find one, when he encountered unexpectedly his old friend, Guy Breddon.

Breddon (that was not his real name) was a man of considerable fortune, a member of the learned societies, and devoted to Central African exploration. He was two or three years younger than the Archdeacon, and a man of tremendous physique.

Breddon was surprised to find the Archdeacon in London, and the Archdeacon was equally surprised to find Breddon in England at all. Breddon carried off the Archdeacon with him to his rooms, and sent a servant in a cab to the Langham to pay the Archdeacon's bill and fetch his luggage. The Archdeacon protested, but faintly, and Breddon would not hear of his hospitality being refused.

Breddon's rooms were an expensive suite immediately over a ruinous upholsterer's in a street off Berkeley Square. There was a private street-door, and from it a private staircase to the first and second floors.

The suite of rooms on the first floor, occupied by Breddon, was entirely shut off from the staircase by a door. The second floor suite, tenanted by an Irish M.P., was similarly shut off, and at that time was unoccupied.

Breddon and the Archdeacon passed through the street-door and up the stairs to the first landing, from whence, by the staircase-door, they entered the flat. Breddon had only recently taken the flat, and the Archdeacon had never been there before. It consisted of a broad L-shaped passage with rooms opening into it. There were many trophies on the walls. Horned heads glared at them; stealthy but stuffed beasts watched them furtively from under tables. There was a perfect arsenal of murderous weapons gleaming brightly under the shaded gaslights.

Breddon's servant prepared supper for them before leaving for the Langham, and soon the two men were discussing Mr Tennyson, Mr Irving, and a parody of the "Queen of the May" which had recently appeared in *Punch*, and doing justice to some oysters, a cold pheasant with an excellent salad, and a bottle of '74 Pommery. It was characteristic of the Archdeacon that he remembered exactly the items of the supper, and that Breddon rather neglected the wine.

After supper they passed into the library, where a bright fire was burning. The Archdeacon walked towards the fire, rubbing his plump hands together. As he did so, a portion of the great rug of grey fur on which he was standing seemed to rise up. It was a grey cat of enormous size, larger than any that the Archdeacon had ever seen before, and of the same colour as the rug on which it had been sleeping. It rubbed itself affectionately against the Archdeacon's leg, and purred as he bent down to stroke it.

"What an extraordinary animal!" said the Archdeacon. "I had no idea cats could grow to this size. Its head's queer, too—so much too small for the body."

"Yes," said Breddon, "and his feet are just as much too big."

The grey cat stretched himself voluptuously under the Archdeacon's caressing hand, and the feet could be seen plainly. They were very broad, and the claws, which shot out, seemed unusually powerful and well developed. The beast's coat was short, thick and wiry.

"Most extraordinary!" the Archdeacon repeated.

He lowered himself into a comfortable chair by the fire. He was still bending over the cat and playing with it when a slight chink made him look up. Breddon was putting something down on the table behind the liquor decanters.

"Any particular breed?" the Archdeacon asked.

"Not that I know of. Freakish, I should say. We found him on board the boat when I left for home—may have come there after mice. He'd have been thrown overboard but for me. I got rather interested in him. Smoke?"

"Oh, thank you."

Outside a cold north wind screamed in quick gusts. Within came the sharp scratch of the match on the ribbed glass as the Archdeacon lit his cigar, the bubble of the rose-water in Breddon's hookah, the soft step of Breddon's man carrying the Archdeacon's luggage into the bedroom at the end of the L-shaped passage, and the constant purring of the big grey cat.

"And what's the cat's name?" the Archdeacon asked.

Breddon laughed.

"Well, if you must have the plain truth, he's called Grey Devil—or, more frequently, Devil *tout court*."

"Really, now, really, you can't expect an Archdeacon to use such abominable language. I shall call him Grey—or perhaps Mr Grey would be more respectful, seeing the shortness of our acquaintance. Do you object to the smell of smoke, Mr Grey? The intelligent beast does not object. Probably you've accustomed him to it."

"Well, seeing what his name is, he could hardly object to smoke, could he?"

Breddon's servant entered. As the door opened and shut, one heard for a moment the crackle of the newly-lit fire in the room that awaited the Archdeacon. The servant swept up the hearth, and, under Archidiaconal direction, mixed a lengthy brandy-and-soda. He retired with the information that he would not be wanted again that night.

"Did you notice," asked the Archdeacon, "the way Mr Grey followed your man about? I never saw a more affectionate cat."

"Think so?" said Breddon. "Watch this time."

For the first time he approached the grey cat, and stretched out his hand as if to pet him. In an instant the cat seemed to have gone mad. Its claws shot out, its back hooped, its coat bristled, its tail stood erect; it cursed and spat, and its small green eyes glared. But a close observer would have noticed that all the time it watched not only Breddon, but also that object which had chinked as Breddon had put it down behind the decanters.

The Archdeacon lay back in his chair and laughed heartily.

"What funny creatures they are, and never so funny as when they lose their tempers! Really, Mr Grey, out of respect to my cloth, you might have refrained from swearing like that. Poor Mr Grey! Poor puss!"

Breddon resumed his seat with a grim smile. The grey cat slowly subsided, and then thrust its head, as though demanding sympathy, into the fat palm of the Archdeacon's dependent hand.

Suddenly the Archdeacon's eye lighted on the object which the cat had been watching, visible now that the servant had displaced the decanters.

"Goodness me!" he exclaimed, "you've got a revolver there."

"That is so," said Breddon.

"Not loaded, I trust?"

"Oh yes, fully loaded."

"But isn't that very dangerous?"

"Well, no; I'm used to these things, and I'm not careless with them. I should have thought it more dangerous to have introduced Grey Devil to you without it. He's much more powerful than an ordinary cat, and I fancy there's something beside cat in his pedigree. When I bring a stranger to see him I keep the cat covered with the revolver until I see how the land lies. To do the brute justice, he has always been most friendly with everybody except myself. I'm his only antipathy. He'd have gone for me just now but that he's smart enough to be afraid of this."

He tapped the revolver.

"I see," said the Archdeacon seriously, "and can guess how it happened. You scared him one day by firing the revolver for a joke; the report frightened him, and he's never forgiven you or forgotten the revolver. Wonderful memory some of these animals have!"

"Yes," said Breddon, "but that guess won't do. I have never, intentionally or by chance, given the 'Devil' any reason for his enmity. So far as I know he has never heard a firearm, and certainly he has never heard one since I made his acquaintance. Somebody may have scared him before, and I'm inclined to think that somebody did, for there can be no doubt that the brute knows all that a cat need know about a revolver, and that he's scared of it.

"The first time we met was almost in darkness. I'd got some cases that I was particular about, and the captain had said I could go down to look after them. Well, this beast suddenly came out of a lump of black and flew at me. I didn't even recognize that it was a cat, because he's so mighty big. I fetched him a clip on the side of the head that knocked him off, and whipped out my iron. He was away in a streak. He knew. And I've had plenty of proof since that he knows. He'd bite me now if he had the chance, but he understands that he hasn't got the chance. I'm often half inclined to take him on plain—shooting barred—and to feel my own hands breaking his damned neck!"

"Really, old man, really!" said the Archdeacon in perfunctory protest, as he rose and mixed himself another drink.

"Sorry to use strong language, but I don't love that cat, you know."

The Archdeacon expressed his surprise that in that case Breddon did not get rid of the brute.

"You come across him on board ship and he flies at you. You save his life, give him board and lodging, and he still hates you so much that he won't let you touch him, and you are no fonder of him than he is of you. Why don't you part company?"

"As for his board, I've rarely known him to eat anything except his own kill. He goes out hunting every night. I keep him simply and solely because I'm afraid of him. As long as I can keep him I know my nerves are all right. If I let my funk of him make any difference—well, I shouldn't be much good in a Central African forest. At first I had some idea of taming him—and, besides, there was a queer coincidence."

He rose and opened the window, and Grey Devil slowly slunk up to it. He paused a few moments on the window-sill and then suddenly sprang and vanished.

"What was the coincidence?"

"What do you think of that?"

Breddon handed the Archdeacon a figure of a cat which he had taken from the mantelpiece. It was a little thing about three inches high. In colour, in the small head, enormous feet, and curiously human eyes, it seemed an exact reproduction of Grey Devil.

"A perfect likeness. How did you get it made?"

"I got the likeness before I got the original. A little Jew dealer sold it me the night before I left for England. He thought it was Egyptian, and described it as an idol. Anyhow, it was a nicish piece of jade."

"I always thought jade was bright green."

"It may be—or white—or brown. It varies. I don't think there can be any doubt that this little figure is old, though I doubt if it's Egyptian."

Breddon put it back in its place.

"By the way, that same night the little Jew came to try and buy it back again. He offered me twice what I had given for it. I said he must have found somebody who was pretty keen on it. I asked if it was a collector. The Jew thought not; said it was a coloured gentleman. Well, that finished it. I wasn't going to do anything to oblige a nigger. The Jew pleaded that it was a particularly fine buck-nigger, with mountains of money, who'd been tracking the thing for years, and hinted at all manner of mumbo-jumbo business—to scare me, I suppose. However, I wouldn't listen, and kicked him out. Then came the coincidence. Having bought the likeness, next day I found the living original. Rum, wasn't it?"

At this moment the clock struck, and the Archdeacon recognized with horror that it was very, very much past the time when respectable Archdeacons should be in bed and asleep. He rose and said goodnight, observing that he'd like to hear more about it on the morrow.

This was extremely unfortunate, for it will be seen it is just at this part of the story that one wants full details, and on the morrow it became impossible to elicit them.

Before leaving the library Breddon closed the window, and the

Archdeacon asked how "Mr Grey", as he called him, would get back.

"Very likely he's back already. He's got a special window in the kitchen, made on purpose, just big enough to let him get in and out as he likes."

"But don't other cats get in, too?"

"No," said Breddon. "Other cats avoid Grey Devil."

The Archdeacon found himself unaccountably nervous when he got to his room. He owned to me that he had to satisfy himself that there was no one concealed under the bed or in the wardrobe. However, he got into bed, and after a little while fell into a deep sleep; his fire was burning brightly, and the room was quite light.

Shortly after four he was awakened by a loud scream. Still sleepy, he did not for the moment locate the sound, thinking that it must have come from the street outside. But almost immediately afterwards he heard the report of a revolver fired twice in quick succession, and then, after a short pause, a third time.

The Archdeacon was terribly frightened. He did not know what had happened, and thought of armed burglars. For a time—he did not think it could have been more than a minute—fear held him motionless. Then with an effort he rose, lit the gas, and hurried on his clothes. As he was dressing, he heard a step down the passage and a knock at his door.

He opened it, and found Breddon's servant. The man had put on a blue overcoat over his night-things, and wore slippers. He was shivering with cold and terror.

"Oh, my God, sir!" he exclaimed, "Mr Breddon's shot himself. Would you come, sir?"

The Archdeacon followed the man to Breddon's bedroom. The smoke still hung thickly in the room. A mirror had been smashed, and lay in fragments on the floor. On the bed, with his back to the Archdeacon, lay Breddon, dead. His right hand still grasped the revolver, and there was a blackened wound behind the right ear.

When the Archdeacon came round to look at the face he turned faint, and the servant took him out into the library and gave him brandy, the glasses and decanters still standing there. Breddon's face certainly had looked very ghastly; it had been scratched, torn and bitten; one eye was gone, and the whole face was covered with blood.

"Do you think it was that brute did it?"

"Sure of it, sir; sprang on his face while he was asleep. I knew it would happen one of these nights. He knew it too; always slept with the revolver by his side. He fired twice at the brute, but couldn't see for the blood. Then he killed himself."

It seemed likely enough, with his eyesight gone, horribly mauled, in an agony of pain, possibly believing that he was saving himself from a death still more horrible, Breddon might very well have turned the weapon on himself.

"What do we do now?" the man asked.

"We must get a doctor and fetch the police at once. Come on."

As they turned the corner of the passage, they saw that the door communicating with the staircase was open.

"Did you open that door?" asked the Archdeacon.

"No," said the man, aghast.

"Then who did?"

"Don't know, sir. Looks as if we weren't at the end of this yet."

They passed down the stairs together, and found the street-door also ajar. On the pavement outside lay a policeman slowly recovering consciousness. Breddon's man took the policeman's whistle and blew it. A passing hansom, going back to the mews, slowed up, the cab was sent to fetch a doctor, and communication with the police-station rapidly followed.

The injured policeman told a curious story. He was passing the house when he heard shots fired. Almost immediately afterwards he heard the bolts of the front-door being drawn, and stepped back into the neighbouring doorway. The front-door opened, and a negro emerged clad in a grey tweed suit with a grey overcoat. The policeman jumped out, and without a second's hesitation the black man felled him. "It was all done before you could think," was the policeman's phrase.

"What kind of negro?" asked the Archdeacon.

"A big man—stood over six foot, and black as coal. He never waited to be challenged; the moment he knew that he was seen he hit out."

The policeman was not a very intelligent fellow, and there was little more to be got out of him. He had heard the shots, seen the street-door open and the man in grey appear, and had been felled by a lightning blow before he had time to do anything.

The doctor, a plain, matter-of-fact little man, had no hesitation in saying that Breddon was dead, and must have died almost immediately. After the injuries received, respiration and heart-action must have ceased at once. He was explaining something which oozed from the dead man's ear, when the Archdeacon could stand it no longer, and staggered out into the library. There he found Breddon's servant, still in the blue overcoat, explaining to a policeman with a notebook that as far as he knew nothing was missing except a jade image or idol of a cat which formerly stood on the mantelpiece.

The cat known as "Grey Devil" was also missing, and, although a description of it was circulated in the public press, nothing was ever heard of it again. But grey fur was found in the clenched left hand of the dead man.

The inquest resulted in the customary verdict, and brought to light no new facts. But it may be as well to give what the police theory of the case was. According to the police the suicide took place much as Breddon's servant had supposed. Mad with pain and unable to bear the thought of his awful mutilation, Breddon had shot himself.

The story of the jade image, as far as it was known, was told at the inquest. The police held that this image was an idol, that some uncivilized tribe was much perturbed by the theft of it, and was ready to pay an enormously high price for its recovery. The negro was assumed to be aware of this, and to have determined to obtain possession of the idol by fair means or foul. Fair means failing, it was suggested that the negro followed Breddon to England, tracked him out, and on the night in question found some means to conceal himself in Breddon's flat. There it was assumed that he fell asleep, was awakened by the screams and the sound of the firing, and, being scared, caught up the jade image and made off. Realizing that the shots would have been heard outside, and that his departure at that moment would be considered extremely suspicious, he was ready as he opened the street-door to fell the first man that he saw. The temporary unconsciousness of the policeman gave him time to get away.

The theory sounds at first sight like the only possible theory. When the Archdeacon first told me the story I tried to find out indirectly whether he accepted it. Finding him rather disposed to fence with my hints and suggestions, I put the question to him plainly and bluntly:

"Do you believe in the police theory?"

He hesitated, and then answered with complete frankness:

"No, most emphatically not."

"Why?" I asked; and he went over the evidence with me.

"In the first place, I do not believe that Breddon, in the ordinary sense, committed suicide. No amount of physical pain would have made him even think of it. He had unending pluck. He would have taken the facial disfigurement and loss of sight as the chances of war, and would have done the best that could be done by a man with such awful disabilities. One must admit that he fired the fatal shot—the medical evidence on that point is too strong to be gainsaid —but he fired it under circumstances of supernatural horror of which we, thank God! know nothing."

"I'm naturally slow to admit supernatural explanation."

"Well, let's go on. What's this mysterious tribe the police talk about? I want to know where it lives and what its name is. It's wealthy enough to offer a huge reward; it must be of some import- ance. The negro managed to get in and secrete himself. How? Where?? I know the flat, and that theory won't do. We don't even know that it was the negro who took that little image, though I believe it was. Anyhow, how did the negro get away at that hour of the morning absolutely unobserved? Negroes are not so common in London that they can walk about without being noticed; yet not one trace of him was ever found, and equally mysterious is the dis- appearance of the Grey Cat. It was such an extraordinary brute, and the description of it was so widely circulated that it would have seemed almost certain we should hear of it again. Well, we've not heard."

We discussed the police theory for some little time, and something which he happened to say led me to exclaim:

"Really! Do you mean to say that the Grey Cat actually was the negro?"

"No," he replied, "not exactly that, but something near it. Cats are strange animals, anyhow. I needn't remind you of their connection with certain old religions or with that witchcraft in which even in England today some still believe, and not so long ago almost all believed. I have never, by the way, seen a good explanation of the fact that there are people who cannot bear to be in a room with a cat, and are aware of its presence as if by some mysterious extra sense. Let me remind you of the belief which undoubtedly exists both in China and Japan, that evil spirits may enter into certain of the lower animals, the fox and badger especially. Every student of demonology knows about these things.

"But that idea of evil spirits taking possession of cats or foxes is surely a heathen superstition which you cannot hold."

"Well, I have read of the evil spirits that entered into the swine. Think it over, and keep an open mind."

THE KING OF THE CATS

by Stephen Vincent Benét

A TWO-TIME WINNER *of the Pulitzer Prize for Poetry, Stephen Vincent Benét (1898–1943) was an undoubted American master of the short story, achieving a perfection in that medium which his novels never attained. His writing did much towards the establishment of an American sense of folk-lore and his stories are often touched with a humour that is at once gentle, wry and innocently earthy, an effect that can best be described as indigenously American.*

Benét was often attracted to fantasy and particularly to American folk-legends for his subject matter. He was one of the first writers to predict the horrors of atomic warfare, describing (in By the Waters of Babylon) *the ruins of New York after* The Bomb *has dropped. One of his best stories,* The Devil and Daniel Webster, *was made into a classic film and another story,* Johnny Pye and the Fool Killer, *has been filmed with Anthony Perkins.*

The following story is typical Benét: delicate, biting, brilliant.

"But, my *dear*," said Mrs Culverin, with a tiny gasp, "you can't actually mean—a *tail*!"

Mrs Dingle nodded impressively. "Exactly. I've seen him. Twice. Paris, of course, and then, a command appearance at Rome—we were in the Royal box. He conducted—my dear, you've never heard such effects from an orchestra—and, my dear," she hesitated slightly, "he conducted *with it*."

"How perfectly, fascinatingly too horrid for words!" said Mrs

Culverin in a dazed but greedy voice. "We *must* have him to dinner as soon as he comes over—he is coming over, isn't he?"

"The twelfth," said Mrs Dingle with a gleam in her eyes. "The New Symphony people have asked him to be guest-conductor for three special concerts—I do hope you can dine with *us* some night while he's here—he'll be very busy, of course—but he's promised to give us what time he can spare—"

"Oh, thank you, dear," said Mrs Culverin, abstractedly, her last raid upon Mrs Dingle's pet British novelist still fresh in her mind. "You're always so delightfully hospitable—but you mustn't wear yourself out—the rest of us must do *our* part—I know Henry and myself would be only too glad to—"

"That's very sweet of you, darling." Mrs Dingle also remembered the larceny of the British novelist. "But we're just going to give Monsieur Tibault—sweet name, isn't it! They say he's descended from the Tybalt in 'Romeo and Juliet' and that's why he doesn't like Shakespeare—we're just going to give Monsieur Tibault the simplest sort of time—a little reception after his first concert, perhaps. He hates," she looked around the table, "large, mixed parties. And then, of course, his—er—little idiosyncrasy—" she coughed delicately. "It makes him feel a trifle shy with strangers."

"But I don't understand yet, Aunt Emily," said Tommy Brooks, Mrs Dingle's nephew. "Do you really mean this Tibault bozo has a tail? Like a monkey and everything?"

"Tommy dear," said Mrs Culverin, crushingly, "in the first place, Monsieur Tibault is not a bozo—he is a very distinguished musician —the finest conductor in Europe. And in the second place—"

"He has," Mrs Dingle was firm. "He has a tail. He conducts with it."

"Oh, but honestly!" said Tommy, his ears pinkening. "I mean— of course, if you say so, Aunt Emily, I'm sure he has—but still, it sounds pretty steep, if you know what I mean! How about it, Professor Tatto?"

Professor Tatto cleared his throat. "Tck," he said, putting his fingertips together cautiously, "I shall be very anxious to see this Monsieur Tibault. For myself, I have never observed a genuine specimen of *homo caudatus*, so I should be inclined to doubt, and yet ... In the Middle Ages, for instance, the belief in men—er—tailed or with caudal appendages of some sort, was both widespread and, as far as we can gather, well founded. As late as the eighteenth century, a Dutch sea-captain with some character for veracity recounts the discovery of a pair of such creatures in the island of Formosa. They were in a low state of civilization, I believe, but the appendages in question were quite distinct. And in 1860, Dr Grimbrook, the English surgeon, claims to have treated no less than three African natives with short but evident tails—though his testimony rests upon his unsupported word. After all, the thing is not impossible, though doubtless unusual. Web feet—rudimentary gills—these occur with some frequency. The appendix we have with us always. The chain of our descent from the ape-like form is by no means complete. For that matter," he beamed around the table, "what can we call the last few vertebrae of the normal spine but the beginnings of a concealed and rudimentary tail? Oh, yes—yes—it's possible—quite—that in an extraordinary case—a reversion of type—a survival—though, of course—"

"I told you so," said Mrs Dingle triumphantly. "*Isn't* it fascinating? Isn't it, Princess?"

The Princess Vivrakanarda's eyes, blue as a field of larkspur, fathomless as the centre of heaven, rested lightly for a moment on Mrs Dingle's excited countenance.

"Ve-ry fascinating," she said, in a voice like stroked, golden velvet. "I should like—I should like ve-ry much to meet this Monsieur Tibault."

"Well, *I* hope he breaks his neck!" said Tommy Brooks, under his breath—but nobody ever paid much attention to Tommy.

Nevertheless as the time for Mr Tibault's arrival in these States drew nearer and nearer, people in general began to wonder whether the Princess had spoken quite truthfully—for there was no doubt of the fact that, up till then, she had been the unique sensation of the season—and you know what social lions and lionesses are.

It was, if you remember, a Siamese season, and genuine Siamese were at quite as much of a premium as Russian accents had been in the quaint old days when the Chauve-Souris was a novelty. The Siamese Art Theatre, imported at terrific expense, was playing to packed houses. *Gushuptzgu,* an epic novel of Siamese farm life, in nineteen closely-printed volumes, had just been awarded the Nobel prize. Prominent pet-and-newt dealers reported no cessation in the appalling demand for Siamese cats. And upon the crest of this wave of interest in things Siamese, the Princess Vivrakanarda poised with the elegant nonchalance of a Hawaiian water-baby upon its surf-board. She was indispensable. She was incomparable. She was every-where.

Youthful, enormously wealthy, allied on one hand to the Royal Family of Siam and on the other to the Cabots (and yet with the first eighteen of her twenty-one years shrouded from speculation in a golden zone of mystery), the mingling of races in her had pro-duced an exotic beauty as distinguished as it was strange. She moved with a feline, effortless grace, and her skin was as if it had been gently powdered with tiny grains of the purest gold—yet the blue-ness of her eyes, set just a trifle slantingly, was as pure and startling as the sea on the rocks of Maine. Her brown hair fell to her knees— she had been offered extraordinary sums by the Master Barbers' Protective Association to have it shingled. Straight as a waterfall tumbling over brown rocks, it had a vague perfume of sandalwood and suave spices and held tints of rust and the sun. She did not talk very much—but then she did not have to—her voice had an odd, small, melodious huskiness that haunted the mind. She lived alone and was reputed to be very lazy—at least it was known that she slept during most of the day—but at night she bloomed like a moon-flower and a depth came into her eyes.

It was no wonder that Tommy Brooks fell in love with her. The wonder was that she let him. There was nothing exotic or distin-guished about Tommy—he was just one of those pleasant, normal young men who seem created to carry on the bond business by read-ing the newspapers in the University Club during most of the day, and can always be relied upon at night to fill an unexpected hole in a dinner-party. It is true that the Princess could hardly be said to do more than tolerate any of her suitors—no one had ever seen those aloofly arrogant eyes enliven at the entrance of any male. But she seemed to be able to tolerate Tommy a little more than the rest— and that young man's infatuated day-dreams were beginning to be beset by smart solitaires and imaginary apartments on Park Avenue, when the famous M Tibault conducted his first concert at Carnegie Hall.

Tommy Brooks sat beside the Princess. The eyes he turned upon her were eyes of longing and love, but her face was as impassive as a mask, and the only remark she made during the preliminary bust-lings was that there seemed to be a number of people in the audience. But Tommy was relieved, if anything, to find her even a little more aloof than usual, for, ever since Mrs Culverin's dinner-party, a vague disquiet as to the possible impression which this Tibault creature might make upon her had been growing in his mind. It shows his devotion that he was present at all. To a man whose simple Princetonian nature found in "Just a Little Love, a Little Kiss", the quintessence of musical art, the average symphony was a positive torture, and he looked forward to the evening's pro-gramme itself with a grim, brave smile.

"Ssh!" said Mrs Dingle, breathlessly. "He's coming!" It seemed to the startled Tommy as if he were suddenly back in the trenches under a heavy barrage, as M Tibault made his entrance to a perfect bombardment of applause.

Then the enthusiastic noise was sliced off in the middle and a gasp took its place—a vast, windy sigh, as if every person in that multitude had suddenly said, "Ah". For the papers had not lied about him. The tail was there.

They called him theatric—but how well he understood the uses of theatricalism! Dressed in unrelieved black from head to foot (the black dress-shirt had been a special token of Mussolini's esteem), he did not walk on, he strolled, leisurely, easily, aloofly, the famous tail curled nonchalantly about one wrist—a suave, black panther loung-ing through a summer garden with that little mysterious weave of the head that panthers have when they pad behind bars—the glittering darkness of his eyes unmoved by any surprise or elation. He nodded, twice, in regal acknowledgement, as the clapping reached an apogee of frenzy. To Tommy there was something dreadfully reminiscent of the Princess in the way he nodded. Then he turned to his orchestra.

A second and louder gasp went up from the audience at this

point, for, as he turned, the tip of that incredible tail twined with dainty carelessness into some hidden pocket and produced a black baton. But Tommy did not even notice. He was looking at the Princess instead.

She had not even bothered to clap, at first, but now—he had never seen her moved like this, never. She was not applauding, her hands were clenched in her lap, but her whole body was rigid, rigid as a steel bar, and the blue flowers of her eyes were bent upon the figure of M Tibault in a terrible concentration. The pose of her entire figure was so still and intense that for an instant Tommy had the lunatic idea that any moment she might leap from her seat beside him as lightly as a moth, and land, with no sound, at M Tibault's side to—yes—to rub her proud head against his coat in worship. Even Mrs Dingle would notice in a moment.

"Princess—" he said, in a horrified whisper, "Princess—"

Slowly the tenseness of her body relaxed, her eyes veiled again, she grew calm.

"Yes, Tommy?" she said, in her usual voice, but there was still something about her . . .

"Nothing, only—oh, hang—he's starting!" said Tommy, as M Tibault, his hands loosely clasped before him, turned and *faced* the audience. His eyes dropped, his tail switched once impressively, then gave three little preliminary taps with his baton on the floor.

Seldom has Gluck's overture to "Iphigenie in Aulis" received such an ovation. But it was not until the Eighth Symphony that the hysteria of the audience reached its climax. Never before had the New Symphony played so superbly—and certainly never before had it been led with such genius. Three prominent conductors in the audience were sobbing with the despairing admiration of envious children towards the close, and one at least was heard to offer wildly ten thousand dollars to a well-known facial surgeon there present for a shred of evidence that tails of some variety could by any stretch of science be grafted upon a normally decaudate form. There was no doubt about it—no mortal hand and arm, be they ever so dexterous, could combine the delicate elan and powerful grace displayed in every gesture of M Tibault's tail.

A sable staff, it dominated the brasses like a flicker of black lightning; an ebon, elusive whip, it drew the last exquisite breath of melody from the woodwinds and ruled the stormy strings like a magician's rod. M Tibault bowed and bowed again—roar after roar of frenzied admiration shook the hall to its foundations—and when he finally staggered, exhausted, from the platform, the president of the Wednesday Sonata Club was only restrained by force from flinging her ninety-thousand-dollar string of pearls after him in an excess of aesthetic appreciation. New York had come and seen— and New York was conquered. Mrs Dingle was immediately besieged by reporters, and Tommy Brooks looked forward to the "little party" at which he was to meet the new hero of the hour with feelings only a little less lugubrious than those that would have come to him just before taking his seat in the electric chair.

The meeting between his Princess and M Tibault was worse and better than he expected. Better because, after all, they did not say much to each other—and worse because it seemed to him, somehow, that some curious kinship of mind between them made words unnecessary. They were certainly the most distinguished-looking couple in the room, as he bent over her hand. "So darlingly foreign, both of them, and yet so different," babbled Mrs Dingle—but Tommy couldn't agree.

They were different, yes—the dark, lithe stranger with the bizarre appendage tucked carelessly in his pocket, and the blue-eyed, brown-haired girl. But that difference only accentuated what they had in common—something in the way they moved, in the suavity of their gestures, in the set of their eyes. Something deeper, even, than race. He tried to puzzle it out—then, looking around at the others, he had a flash of revelation. It was as if that couple were foreign, indeed—not only to New York but to all common humanity. As if they were polite guests from a different star.

Tommy did not have a very happy evening, on the whole. But his mind worked slowly, and it was not until much later that the mad suspicion came upon him in full force.

Perhaps he is not to be blamed for his lack of immediate comprehension. The next few weeks were weeks of bewildered misery for him. It was not that the Princess's attitude towards him had changed—she was just as tolerant of him as before, but M Tibault was always there. He had a faculty of appearing, as out of thin air—he walked, for all his height, as lightly as a butterfly—and Tommy grew to hate the faintest shuffle on the carpet that announced his presence.

And then, hang it all, the man was so smooth, so infernally, unruffably smooth! He was never out of temper, never embarrassed. He treated Tommy with the extreme of urbanity, and yet his eyes mocked, deep-down, and Tommy could do nothing. And, gradually, the Princess become more and more drawn to this stranger, in a soundless communion that found little need for speech—and that, too, Tommy saw and hated, and that, too, he could not mend.

He began to be haunted not only by M Tibault in the flesh, but by M Tibault in the spirit. He slept badly, and when he slept, he dreamed—of M Tibault, a man no longer, but a shadow, a spectre, the limber ghost of an animal whose words came purringly between sharp little pointed teeth. There was certainly something odd about the whole shape of the fellow—his fluid ease, the mould of his head, even the cut of his fingernails—but just what it was escaped Tommy's intensest cogitation. And when he did put his finger on it at length, at first he refused to believe.

A pair of petty incidents decided him, finally, against all reason. He had gone to Mrs Dingle's, one winter afternoon, hoping to find the Princess. She was out with his aunt, but was expected back for tea, and he wandered idly into the library to wait. He was just about to switch on the lights, for the library was always dark even in summer, when he heard a sound of light breathing that seemed to come from the leather couch in the corner. He approached it cautiously and dimly made out the form of M Tibault, curled up on the couch, peacefully asleep.

The sight annoyed Tommy so that he swore under his breath and was back near the door on his way out, when the feeling we all know and hate, the feeling that eyes we cannot see are watching us, arrested him. He turned back—M Tibault had not moved a muscle of his body to all appearance—but his eyes were open now. And those eyes were black and human no longer. They were green—Tommy could have sworn it—and he could have sworn that they had no bottom and gleamed like little emeralds in the dark. It only lasted a moment, for Tommy pressed the light-button automatically—and there was M Tibault, his normal self, yawning a little but urbanely apologetic, but it gave Tommy time to think. Nor did what happened a trifle later increase his peace of mind.

They had lit a fire and were talking in front of it—by now Tommy hated M Tibault so thoroughly that he felt that odd yearning for his company that often occurs in such cases. M Tibault was telling some anecdote and Tommy was hating him worse than ever for basking with such obvious enjoyment in the heat of the flames and the ripple of his own voice.

Then they heard the street-door open, and M Tibault jumped up —and jumping, caught one sock on a sharp corner of the brass fire-rail and tore it open in a jagged flap. Tommy looked down mechanically at the tear—a second's glace, but enough—for M Tibault, for the first time in Tommy's experience, lost his temper completely. He swore violently in some spitting, foreign tongue—his face distorted suddenly—he clapped his hand over his sock. Then, glaring furiously at Tommy, he fairly sprang from the room, and Tommy could hear him scaling the stairs in long, agile bounds.

Tommy sank into a chair, careless for once of the fact that he heard the Princess's light laugh in the hall. He didn't want to see the Princess. He didn't want to see anybody. There had been something revealed when M Tibault had torn that hole in his sock —and it was not the skin of a man. Tommy had caught a glimpse of—black plush. Black velvet. And then had come M Tibault's sudden explosion of fury. Good *Lord*—did the man wear black velvet stockings under his ordinary socks? Or could he—could he— but here Tommy held his fevered head in his hands.

He went to Professor Tatto that evening with a series of hypothetical questions, but as he did not dare confide his real suspicions to the Professor, the hypothetical answers he received served only to confuse him the more. Then he thought of Billy Strange. Billy was a good sort, and his mind had a turn for the bizarre. Billy might be able to help.

He couldn't get hold of Billy for three days and lived through the interval in a fever of impatience. But finally they had dinner together at Billy's apartment, where his queer books were, and Tommy was able to blurt out the whole disordered jumble of his suspicions.

Billy listened without interrupting until Tommy was quite through. Then he pulled at his pipe. "But, my dear *man*—" he said, protestingly.

"Oh, I know—I know—" said Tommy, and waved his hands, "I know I'm crazy—you needn't tell me that—but I tell you, the man's a cat all the same—no, I don't see how he could be, but he is—why, hang it, in the first place, everybody knows he's got a tail!"

"Even so," said Billy, puffing. "Oh, my dear Tommy, I don't doubt you saw, or think you saw, everything you say. But, even so—" He shook his head.

"But what about those other birds, werewolves and things?" said Tommy.

Billy looked dubious. "We-ll," he admitted, "you've got me there, of course. At least—a tailed man *is* possible. And the yarns about werewolves go back far enough, so that—well, I wouldn't say there aren't or haven't been werewolves—but then I'm willing to believe more things than most peolpe. But a were-cat—or a man that's a cat and a cat that's a man—honestly, Tommy—"

"If I don't get some real advice I'll go clean off my hinge. For Heaven's sake, tell me something to *do*!"

"Lemme think," said Billy. "First, you're pizen-sure this man is—"

"A cat. Yeah," and Tommy nodded violently.

"Check. And second—if it doesn't hurt your feelings. Tommy—you're afraid this girl you're in love with has—er—at least a streak of—felinity—in her—and so she's drawn to him?"

"Oh, Lord, Billy, if I only knew!"

"Well—er—suppose she really is, too, you know—would you still be keen on her?"

"I'd marry her if she turned into a dragon every Wednesday!" said Tommy, fervently.

Billy smiled. "H'm," he said, "then the obvious thing to do is to get rid of this M Tibault. Lemme think."

He thought about two pipes full, while Tommy sat on pins and needles. Then, finally, he burst out laughing.

"What's so darn funny?" said Tommy, aggrievedly.

"Nothing, Tommy, only I've just thought of a stunt—something so blooming crazy—but if he is—h'm—what you think he is—it *might* work—" And, going to the book-case, he took down a book.

"If you think you're going to quiet my nerves by reading me a bedtime story—"

"Shut up, Tommy, and listen to this—if you really want to get rid of your feline friend."

"What is it?"

"Book of Agnes Repplier's. About cats. Listen."

" 'There is also a Scandinavian version of the ever famous story which Sir Walter Scott told to Washington Irving, which Monk Lewis told to Shelley and which, in one form or another, we find embodied in the folklore of every land'—now, Tommy, pay attention—'the story of the traveller who saw within a ruined abbey, a procession of cats, lowering into a grave a little coffin with a crown upon it. Filled with horror, he hastened from the spot; but when he had reached his destination, he could not forbear relating to a friend the wonder he had seen. Scarcely had the tale been told when his friend's cat, who lay curled up tranquilly by the fire, sprang to its feet, cried out, "Then I am the King of the Cats!" and disappeared in a flash up the chimney.' "

"Well?" said Billy, shutting the book.

"By gum!" said Tommy, staring. "By gum! Do you think there's a chance?"

"*I* think we're both in the booby-hatch. But if you want to try it—"

"Try it! I'll spring it on him the next time I see him. But—listen—I can't make it a ruined abbey—"

"Oh, use your imagination! Make it Central Park—anywhere. Tell it as if it happened to you—seeing the funeral procession and all that. You can lead into it somehow—let's see—some general line —oh, yes—'Strange, isn't it, how fact so often copies fiction. Why, only yesterday—' See?"

"Strange, isn't it, how fact so often copies fiction," repeated Tommy dutifully. "Why, only yesterday—"

"I happened to be strolling through Central Park when I saw something very odd."

"I happened to be strolling through—here, gimme that book!" said Tommy, "I want to learn the rest of it by heart!"

Mrs Dingle's farewell dinner to the famous Monsieur Tibault, on the occasion of his departure for his Western tour, was looked forward to with the greatest expectations. Not only would everybody be there, including the Princess Vivrakanarda, but Mrs Dingle, a hinter if there ever was one, had let it be known that at this dinner an announcement of very unusual interest to Society might be made. So everyone, for once, was almost on time, except for Tommy. He was at least fifteen minutes early, for he wanted to have speech with his aunt alone. Unfortunately, however, he had hardly taken off his overcoat when she was whispering some news in his ear so rapidly that he found it difficult to understand a word of it.

"And you mustn't breathe it to a soul!" she ended, beaming. "That is, not before the announcement—I think we'll have *that* with the salad—people never pay very much attention to salad—"

"Breathe what, Aunt Emily?" said Tommy, confused.

"The Princess, darling—the dear Princess and Monsieur Tibault —they just got engaged this afternoon, dear things! Isn't it *fascinating?*"

"Yeah," said Tommy, and started to walk blindly through the nearest door. His aunt restrained him.

"Not there, dear—not in the library. You can congratulate them later. They're just having a sweet little moment alone there now—" And she turned away to harry the butler, leaving Tommy stunned.

But his chin came up after a moment. He wasn't beaten yet.

"Strange, isn't it, how often fact copies fiction?" he repeated to himself in dull mnemonics, and, as he did so, he shook his fist at the library door.

Mrs Dingle was wrong, as usual. The Princess and M Tibault were not in the library—they were in the conservatory, as Tommy discovered when he wandered aimlessly past the glass doors.

He didn't mean to look, and after a second he turned away. But that second was enough.

Tibault was seated in a chair and she was crouched on a stool at his side, while his hand, softly, smoothly, stroked her brown hair. Black cat and Siamese kitten. Her face was hidden from Tommy, but he could see Tibault's face. And he could hear.

They were not talking, but there was a sound between them. A warm and contented sound like the murmur of giant bees in a hollow tree—a golden, musical rumble, deep-throated, that came from Tibault's lips and was answered by hers—a golden purr.

Tommy found himself back in the drawing-room, shaking hands with Mrs Culverin, who said, frankly, that she had seldom seen him look so pale.

The first two courses of the dinner passed Tommy like dreams, but Mrs Dingle's cellar was notable, and by the middle of the meat course, he began to come to himself. He had only one resolve now.

For the next few moments he tried desperately to break into the conversation, but Mrs Dingle was talking, and even Gabriel will have a time interrupting Mrs Dingle. At last, though, she paused for breath and Tommy saw his chance.

"Speaking of that," said Tommy, piercingly, without knowing in the least what he was referring to, "Speaking of that—"

"As I was saying," said Professor Tatto. But Tommy would not yield. The plates were being taken away. It was time for salad.

"Speaking of that," he said again, so loudly and strangely that Mrs Culverin jumped and an awkward hush fell over the table. "Strange, isn't it, how often fact copies fiction?" There, he was startled. His voice rose even higher. "Why, only today I was strolling through—" and, word for word, he repeated his lesson. He could see Tibault's eyes glowing at him, as he described the funeral. He could see the Princess, tense.

He could not have said what he had expected might happen when he came to the end; but it was not bored silence, everywhere, to be followed by Mrs Dingle's acrid, "Well, Tommy, is that *quite* all?"

He slumped back in his chair, sick at heart. He was a fool and his last resource had failed. Dimly he heard his aunt's voice, saying,

"Well, then—" and realized that she was about to make the fatal announcement.

But just then Monsieur Tibault spoke.

"One moment, Mrs Dingle," he said, with extreme politeness, and she was silent. He turned to Tommy.

"You are—positive I suppose, of what you saw this afternoon, Brooks?" he said, in tones of light mockery.

"Absolutely," said Tommy sullenly. "Do you think I'd—"

"Oh, no, no, no," Monsieur Tibault waved the implication aside, "but—such an interesting story—one likes to be sure of the details—and, of course, you *are* sure—*quite* sure—that the kind of crown you describe was on the coffin?"

"Of course," said Tommy, wondering, "but—"

"Then I'm the King of the Cats!" cried Monsieur Tibault in a voice of thunder, and, even as he cried it, the houselights blinked—there was the soft thud of an explosion that seemed muffled in cotton-wool from the minstrel gallery—and the scene was lit for a second by an obliterating and painful burst of light that vanished in an instant and was succeeded by heavy, blinding clouds of white, pungent smoke.

"Oh, those *horrid* photographers," came Mrs Dingle's voice in a melodious wail. "I *told* them not to take the flashlight picture till dinner was over, and now they've taken it *just* as I was nibbling lettuce!"

Someone tittered a little nervously. Someone coughed. Then, gradually the veils of smoke dislimned and the green-and-black spots in front of Tommy's eyes died away.

They were blinking at each other like people who have just come out of a cave into brilliant sun. Even yet their eyes stung with the fierceness of that abrupt illumination and Tommy found it hard to make out the faces across the table from him.

Mrs Dingle took command of the half-blinded company with her accustomed poise. She rose, glass in hand. "And now, dear friends," she said in a clear voice, "I'm sure all of us are very happy to—" Then she stopped, open-mouthed, an expression of incredulous horror on her features. The lifted glass began to spill its contents on the tablecloth in a little stream of amber. As she spoke, she had turned directly to Monsieur Tibault's place at the table—and Monsieur Tibault was no longer there.

Some say there was a bursting flash of fire that disappeared up the chimney—some say it was a giant cat that leaped through the window at a bound, without breaking the glass. Professor Tatto puts it down to a mysterious chemical disturbance operating only over M Tibault's chair. The butler, who is pious, believes the devil in person flew away with him, and Mrs Dingle hesitates between witchcraft and a malicious ectoplasm dematerializing on the wrong cosmic plane. But be that as it may, one thing is certain—in the instant of fictive darkness which followed the glare of the flashlight, Monsieur Tibault, the great conductor, disappeared forever from mortal sight, tail and all.

Mrs Culverin swears he was an international burglar and that she was just about to unmask him, when he slipped away under cover of the flashlight smoke, but no one else who sat at that historic dinner-table believes her. No, there are no sound explanations, but Tommy thinks he knows, and he will never be able to pass a cat again without wondering.

Mrs Tommy is quite of her husband's mind regarding cats—she was Gretchen Woolwine, of Chicago—for Tommy told her his whole story, and while she doesn't believe a great deal of it, there is no doubt in her heart that one person concerned in the affair was a *perfect* cat. Doubtless it would have been more romantic to relate how Tommy's daring finally won him his Princess—but, unfortunately, it would not be veracious. For the Princess Vivrakanarda, also, is with us no longer. Her nerves, shattered by the spectacular denouement of Mrs Dingle's dinner, required a sea-voyage, and from that voyage she has never returned to America.

Of course, there are the usual stories—one hears of her, a nun in a Siamese convent, or a masked dancer at Le Jardin de ma Soeur—one hears that she has been murdered in Patagonia or married in Trebizond—but, as far as can be ascertained, not one of these gaudy fables has the slightest basis of fact. I believe that Tommy, in his heart of hearts, is quite convinced that the sea-voyage was only a pretext, and that by some unheard-of means, she has managed to rejoin the formidable Monsieur Tibault, wherever in the world of the visible or the invisible he may be—in fact, that in some ruined city or subterranean palace they reign together now, King and Queen of all the mysterious Kingdom of Cats. But that, of course, is quite impossible.

THE VAMPIRE CAT

(Traditional)

THOSE GREETINGS-CARDS *and prints of delicately-coloured oriental Cats perhaps deceive us into believing that the Cat is a favoured, even revered, animal in Japan. This is not so and the reason for Eastern aversion to Cats lies way back in shadowy legend. Tradition has it that when the Buddha was very ill and in danger of dying, a Cat killed and ate the rat sent to fetch urgent medicine. If that was not bad enough, the Cat affirmed its evil reputation by being the only creature, along with the venomous viper, to refuse to shed tears at the Buddha's funeral. Consequently, Japanese myth and folklore is full of tales of were-cats, witch-cats and other feline fiends. The famous story of the Vampire Cat of Nabéshima is probably the best of them all.*

Many years ago, so the story is told, one of the Princes of Hizen, of the noble House of Nabeshima, fell under the fearful spell of a thirsty Vampire Cat.

Of all the Prince's household, there was no woman more beautiful than the Lady O Toyo whose delicate good looks and soft charms made her the favourite amongst his many concubines. One afternoon the Prince chose to take his pleasure in the palace gardens and, losing all sense of time in each other's arms, he and O Toyo lingered there beneath the pink blossoms until the sun was chased away by darkness. Feeling a sudden chill wind, the couple strolled back towards the palace and so captivated was he by the company of O Toyo, the Prince failed to notice, hidden among creeping shadows, a monstrous Cat stalking them on silent paws.

After many loving embraces, O Toyo took her leave of the Prince and went to her chambers which were set aside in an attractive but lonely part of the palace. In vain she sought to sleep, her slumbers being disturbed by vivid nightmares of the most horrific kind. As a distant muffled bell struck the midnight hour, O Toyo started awake and lay terrified, scarce daring to breathe, for the whole room was throbbing to the sound of a ghastly *purring.*

O Toyo sat upright to discover the cause of that terrible sound and gasped with fear for she found herself staring into a pair of enormous, baleful yellow eyes that regarded her with amusement from only a few feet away. With fearful certainty the outline of a monstrous Cat crouched ready to leap became distinct at the foot of the bed. O Toyo tried to scream but the Monster leapt upon her and, sinking its fangs into her pale throat, shook her as a cat shakes a mouse until she was dead. Then, after lapping dry the blood that gushed from her severed veins, the Vampire Cat clawed a grave in the earth beneath the veranda and there dragged the chewed and bloodless corpse so that none might find it. And when O Toyo was buried, the Cat assumed the shape of the unfortunate girl and so perfect was the transformation that not even the Prince noticed any change.

Nightly, he made love to his beautiful mistress and never once did he suspect that the creature who responded so passionately to his caresses was a foul succubus, the ravager of his true love. And even as the Prince whispered his love of her, the false O Toyo feasted like a leech upon his blood. So it came to pass that the noble Prince, his life-blood being drained away, grew weaker and weaker until his wife and ministers feared that he was dying of some rare and malignant fever and sent for learned doctors to attend him. None of their charms, potions or medications had the slightest effect and the unfortunate Prince, his face pale and drawn, continued to waste away, his only pleasure being the nightly visits of his beloved O Toyo.

A curious and distressing aspect of the Prince's malady was the hideous dreams that afflicted him every night, dreams in which he imagined O Toyo's fair face worm-eaten and mouldering in the grave, or else saw long-fanged imps rising from deepest Hell to torment him. The restless movements and terrible cries which these nightmares inspired in the Prince sorely moved his ministers and they decided to place a guard of a hundred specially-picked *Samurai* around his bed to reassure him so that he might sleep more soundly. Yet each night, shortly before the sounding of ten o'clock, a great weariness pressed down upon each of the guards and they fell into a deep dreamless sleep more profound than that which the fumes of the poppy induce. Then stealthily, would come O Toyo, creeping through their midst, and for a short time the Prince's nightmares would give way to dreams of silken ecstasy while his blood trickled hotly down the throat of the demon Vampire.

Each morning, the guards would awaken to find their lord's condition even worse, yet, no matter how hard they tried to resist, none could fight the strange slumber that nightly veiled their eyes. More concerned than ever for the life of the Prince, three of his most loyal ministers decided to accompany the guards during their vigil and see if they could evade the net of sleep. But by ten o'clock they too had succumbed and the Vampire crept silently past them to its grisly repast so that when they woke in the morning the Prince's condition had again worsened. Dejectedly, the three ministers came together to discuss the situation and all approved the words of their leader, Isahaya Buzen, when he said, "It can be no mere coincidence that shuts the eyes of a hundred alert guards at the same hour every night. Undoubtedly this is the work of some evil spirit that has bewitched the Prince and against whose devilish powers we are helpless. Let us therefore go and consult wise Ruiten, the head priest of the Temple of Miyo. He may know of potent psalms and prayers which may yet save our young Prince's life."

After hearing the request of the ministers, Ruiten graciously agreed to do all in his power to aid the Prince's recovery and immediately embarked on a severe routine of fasting, prayer and the singing of hymns. These endeavours he continued for several days without noticeable improvement in the Prince's condition. Then, one night, after he had offered up the final prayer of the day and was preparing for bed, the old priest thought he heard an unusual noise from outside. Looking out of the window, he observed a young soldier, not much more than twenty years old, bathing himself in water from the nearby well. Thus purified, the young man put his armour back on and piously addressed himself to the serene countenance of the temple Buddha, praying that the Prince might soon be well again. When he had completed his devotions, the soldier prepared to leave but Ruiten stopped him, crying out, "Wait, young warrior, I would speak with you."

Looking up at the priest, the soldier replied, "If that is your wish, holy one, I am happy to oblige."

"Be so kind as to enter, so that we may talk at our ease."

"With pleasure," responded the soldier and he entered the temple as directed.

When they sat facing each other, soldier and priest, Ruiten exclaimed in kindly fashion, "My heart is full of joy to see so loyal a young soldier. I also have been praying for the recovery of His Highness for I am Ruiten, head priest of this Temple and this duty has been entrusted to me. But, tell me, what is your name?"

"Sir, my name is Ito Soda and I am but an infantryman in the service of the Prince. Since His Highness was first taken ill I have greatly wished to help him recover in whatever way I can. But, unfortunately, so lowly a soldier as myself would never be allowed to enter the presence of His Highness. So I have to be content with praying to Buddha for his recovery."

Such an unselfish declaration of loyalty made Ruiten weep to hear it and, afterwards, he related to Ito Soda the details of all he knew concerning the Prince's sickness, especially of the terrible nightmares that tortured him and of the unholy sleep that nightly befell his guards. Grim understanding showed itself in Ito Soda's face as the priest unfolded his tale.

"There is certainly some devilishness at work," he agreed. "If only I could somehow spend a night in the Prince's chamber I would try and fight off this strange sleep and find out what is behind it all."

Ruiten gave him a searching look for a moment, then revealed, "I am on friendly terms with Isahaya Buzen, the Prince's chief minister. Maybe if I tell him of your eagerness to help the Prince, your wish may soon be granted."

The young soldier expressed heartfelt thanks to the bonze for his suggestion, stressing that his concern was in no way motivated by a desire for promotion or other favours. The old priest chuckled at the

young man's enthusiasm and, after agreeing to meet and visit
Isahaya Buzen the following evening, the two men parted company.

At the arranged time, Ito Soda met Ruiten and accompanied him
to the house of Isahaya Buzen, remaining in an ante-chamber whilst
the priest consulted the chief minister.

"Tell me, sir, what news of the Prince?" asked Ruiten. "Is he
any better for the humble prayers I have offered up on his behalf?"

"If anything, *worse*," replied Isahaya Buzen in a despairing tone.
"Without doubt he is the victim of some evil spirit but since the
guards cannot stay awake we have no way of knowing in what form
the demon attacks him." Ruiten smiled. "I believe I have found
just the man to banish this evil for good," he said.

"Who is he?" cried the minister, thinking the priest had obtained
the services of some famous *Samurai* or other hero.

"He is but a young infantryman, Ito Soda by name, yet in all
Nabéshima I am sure there is no more loyal or courageous soldier.
Please grant him permission that he may join the warriors already
guarding His Highness."

Isahaya Buzen was silent for a moment. "It is pleasing," he said
finally, "to hear such praise of a mere foot-soldier—but to allow
such a person into the royal bedchamber is out of the question."

"He has no fine title," admitted the old bonze, "so why not pro-
mote him and then he may freely join the other officers mounting
guard over His Highness?"

"Promotion should be awarded after a deed and not before,"
observed the minister stiffly, yet the light of hope shone in his eyes.
"In any case, let me see this marvellous fellow so that I am better
able to consider his request." Whereupon Ito Soda was shown in and
so impressed was Isahaya Buzen with his kind looks and modest
loyalty that the very same evening the humble infantryman took
his place alongside the hundred highborn officers encircling the
Prince's sick-bed.

To amuse themselves, the *Samurai* spoke boastfully of past battles
and of how *tonight* they would be sure to stay awake. Ito Soda did
not enter into these loud conversations but sat silently watching
over the sleeping Prince whose bloodless features often grimaced as

if he suffered pain. The evening wore on and not once did Ito Soda take his eyes off the ailing Prince until it suddenly struck him that the room was growing deathly quiet. Looking up he saw that, all about him, his companions were one by one falling into a deep and unnatural slumber. His own limbs seemed to grow monstrously heavy as if encased in heaviest armour, and an urgent desire came upon him to close his eyes. Ito Soda put all his strength of will into resisting the urge to sleep—which suddenly appeared as the most wonderful and desirable state imaginable. He pinched and slapped himself yet hardly felt a thing so numb had his body become. The young soldier realised he would have to resort to the harsher methods for which he had earlier equipped himself. With a desperate effort, he spread a length of oiled paper over the sumptuous carpet upon which he sat, Squatting down on the paper, he drew a small, sharp knife from a sheath and without hesitation plunged it into his leg. The wave of pain that hit him cut sharply through the numbing drowsiness. But a few minutes later, he again felt the mask of sleep tightening. Despite piercing agony, Ido Soda twisted the knife in the wound, again and again, until all desire for sleep completely left him. The oiled paper he had spread beneath him prevented his peasant blood from soiling the royal carpets.

So Ito Soda stayed awake whilst all around him slept and presently he had the satisfaction of hearing a far-off bell strike midnight, a sound which no one else in that room had heard for many nights. At once the doors to the Prince's chamber slid open and a dark figure slipped inside and crept silently towards the sleeping Prince. As the apparition drew nearer, Ito Soda was surprised to make out the shape and features of a beautiful woman, the most beautiful he had ever seen. With a smile of anticipation she drew near the helpless Prince—then stepped back, startled, as she noticed Ito Soda awake and watching her every movement.

"Who are you?" she cried. "I've never seen you before."

"My name is Ito Soda and this is my first night on duty."

"Why are you, of all the men here, awake whilst the other sleep?"

"It is not my fault," replied the young soldier, eyeing his visitor suspiciously. "I never was a very sound sleeper."

At this moment, O Toyo—or the demon in her guise—noticed the red stream of blood collecting thickly on the oiled paper. Her eyes blazed and it seemed to Ito Soda that she wet her scarlet lips with the tip of her tongue.

"You are bleeding!" she exclaimed. "What happened to you?"

"Oh, nothing," Ito Soda casually replied. "I was getting to feel rather tired so I stabbed myself to keep awake."

"How brave!" commented the demon, full of rage.

"Such a scratch is hardly worth consideration," returned Ito Soda. The false O Toyo then turned to the Prince and leaned over him, apparently full of concern.

"How is my Lord feeling tonight?"

The Prince stirred but was too feeble to make a reply. Keeping a careful eye on the beautiful woman, Ito Soda rested a hand on the hilt of his deadly curved sword for he was convinced that she had a part in the bewitchment of the Prince and determined to destroy her instantly at the first sign of her witchcraft. Several times O Toyo drew hungrily near to the Prince yet each time she was temped to feast on his blood she felt the eyes of Ito Soda burning into her and, turning, she would see the deadly intent in his expression. So, after a while, she haughtily departed leaving the Prince to sleep peacefully under the watchful gaze of Ito Soda.

In the morning, the hundred officers awoke as usual and when they discovered that a mere common soldier had stabbed himself in order to stay awake, and so bested them all, they felt great loss of face and returned home dismayed. The ministers, however, were delighted at such a courageous action and eagerly consented that Ito Soda should again stand guard the following night, Predictably, by ten o'clock all the guards had fallen fast asleep except Ito Soda who maintained a vigilant watch. As on the previous night, the demon entered the room and approached the helpless victim but was unable to slake its obscene thirst at the Prince's neck because of the wakeful presence of Ito Soda.

Several days passed and because he had not been attacked since his loyal infantryman joined the guard, the health of the Prince grew rapidly better and there was much rejoicing in the palace.

Ito Soda was rewarded by promotion and heaped with honours and was given a fine estate with a castle as his home.

In all this time, the nocturnal visits of O Toyo to the Prince had proved entirely unrewarding to the demon so it stopped coming altogether and from that night onwards, the royal guards were no longer struck down by the mysterious sleep. Ito Soda noticed this coincidence and became fully convinced that O Toyo was the cause of the Prince's distress. He took his suspicions to Isahaya Buzen who listened thoughtfully then asked, "How shall we rid ourselves of this most attractive-looking of Monsters?"

Ito Soda had already thought of a plan.

"Tonight I shall go to her room," said he, "and strive to kill her. I would humbly suggest, though, that you position eight sturdy men outside the doors and windows in case I fail and she tries to escape."

This course of action being agreed upon, Ito Soda waited until nightfall, then presented himself at O Toyo's chambers under the pretence of having a letter from the Prince. Bidding him enter, the false O Toyo asked, "What message does he send?"

"Only this, an expression of his love. Here . . ."

As he spoke, Ito Soda came close to her, reaching inside his cloak as if for the letter—but instead of a letter he drew out a thin flashing dagger and lunged at her. The demon shrieked and leapt back with the speed of a cat. Seizing a pike, it aimed the weapon at the soldier.

"How dare you attack the Prince's favourite!" growled the demon in a voice suddenly no longer like that of O Toyo. The creature lunged but its intended victim adroitly deflected the thrust with his dagger. Again and again, the fiend slashed at Ito Soda with the pike but each time the young infantryman managed to parry the blow. Realizing it had met its match, the demon flung aside the pike and, before the astonished soldier's eyes changed from a desirable woman into a great shaggy cat. The Vampire hissed its hatred at Ito Soda and before the latter could recover his surprise, it had clawed its way up the wall and out on to the roof. Greatly amazed, Isahaya Buzen and his eight men fired muskets at the

Monster but it evaded their aims and disappeared into the darkness.

The Vampire Cat escaped to the mountains where it resumed its evil doings and plagued the folk of that region. Eventually, the Prince of Hizen, now fully recovered thanks to Ito Soda, organized a massive hunt and in this way the Monster was finally run to earth and destroyed.*

* See p. 189.

THE CAT MAN

by Byron Liggett

ONE PET CAN *be most pleasant, even two or three . . . But few people can have resisted a shudder at the thought of some of the kindly old ladies one hears about who live quite alone except for a few dozen voraciously hungry cats. Imagine then, one man all by himself on a desert island that is* seething *with starving cats! This is the unpleasant situation put forward by Byron Liggett, a retired U.S. Army captain.*

The Cat Man originally appeared in Story *which, for years, had a reputation for publishing the best in shorter American fiction. Of all the tales that appeared in its pages, this must be one of the most disturbing.*

Its real name is Tao Atoll, and it still carries that name on some maps. But after the Cat Man came to the Tuamotus, people started calling it "Cat Island", and it has been known by that name ever since.

Cat Island is a crescent-shaped little atoll that lies about seventy miles north-west of Puka-Puka. As far back as anyone can remember, it has been taboo to the native Polynesians. They wouldn't go near it for all the money in the world. I don't know what native superstition put the original hex on it, but everyone knows why it is taboo today. No one—white or Polynesian—visits it now; they wouldn't dare.

I'll never forget the first day I met the Cat Man. Between the World Wars, I was making an easy living running a mail boat among the islands. The mail contract didn't pay much, but I gathered in a nice percentage hauling supplies and picking up a charter job now and then. I was sitting in the Chinaman's at Papeete having my usual, when a native cabbie brought this little gent in to see me.

I liked him the first time I saw him. He was a small, dried-up little fellow, past fifty, I'd say. He had pale blue eyes and a magnificent head of white hair. He was dressed in a grey linen suit and carried a cane which drew attention to his slight rheumatic limp. He had a kind, intelligent face.

The cabbie pointed me out to him and he shuffled over to my table. He seemed relieved to have found me.

"I understand you are Captain Rogers?" he asked.

"That's right,' I said and stood up. "What can I do for you?"

The little guy took the empty chair I waved him to. He folded both hands over his cane and looked at me with an intense, serious expression.

"I'm told you have a boat I might charter."

His manner and the cut of his clothes made me smell money. Instinctively, I began juggling for a bargaining position.

"I have a sloop, sir," I admitted, "but I also have other obligations at present. Just what did you have in mind?"

He must have recognized my pitch, because he didn't seem the least disappointed.

"My name is Foster, Captain," he said, "Gerald W. Foster." He paused, as though waiting for me to recognize the name. When I didn't, he continued, "I'm a writer. I want to charter your boat to take me to Tao Atoll."

"Tao Atoll?" I blurted out. "What in the world do you want to go there for? There's nothing there but palm trees and rats!"

The man was undeterred. "Well, you see, Captain, I've just bought the island and—"

"Bought it?" I said, incredulously.

The little fellow began to get irritated, and I suddenly realized I was stepping on his dream.

"Captain, I didn't seek you out to ask your advice on the matter. I've purchased a twenty-five year lease on the island from the local government, and I intend to live there the rest of my life. I assure you, I've investigated the project thoroughly."

With that I had him pegged. I'd seen others like him come to French Oceania with that same gleam in their eyes. Some of them came to write, some to paint, and some just came in an effort to escape from themselves. *Soif des îles*—thirst for the islands—is the phrase the French have for it.

The little gent went on to explain that he wanted my sloop to haul him to the island and set him up. He wanted me to carry all his supplies, some building materials, and a couple of local carpenters to build him a cabin. He unfolded his plans with the confidence of a man who had planned his project well and who knew exactly what he wanted.

He didn't seem the slightest concerned about expenses. So, when we got down to the financial end of the deal, I quoted him a haggling price one-third over the one I had hoped to get. He staggered me again when he whipped out his chequebook and made out the full amount in advance payment. Like I said, I knew I would like the Cat Man the first time I laid eyes on him!

I had five days in port before I had to start my next mail run to the islands. The natives Mr Foster had hired began loading my boat the next day. He must have spent a fortune for the materials and supplies they were loading on my sloop.

I lined up a couple of Chinese carpenters for the trip, and they beat a stiff price out of me. I could've got native help for a quarter of the price but none of the natives would tackle the tabooed atoll. The Chinks knew that, too, and were out to make a killing. What did I care? After all, it was his money I was spending. This was a cost-plus deal, so far as I was concerned.

I was supervising the stowing of his gear when Foster himself brought the cats aboard. They were just ordinary-looking cats, and he carried them in two net bags slung over his arms.

"What are those things for, Mr Foster?" I asked.

He smiled. "They are my pets, Captain. They'll keep me company in my exile. They could prove useful, too. You said yourself there were lots of rats on Tao."

I shrugged. His answers made a lot of sense, if you happened to like cats, but I don't care for the damned beasts. I looked them over when he dropped them to the deck.

"Some of them look like females," I remarked.

The Cat Man nodded and smiled. "Yes, Captain," he said. "I'm taking four females and two toms. I expect I'll have a nice crop of kittens before long. Don't you think kittens are cute?"

"Guess they are, if you like 'em. You're liable to get more kittens than you bargained for," I added more prophetically than I realized.

The weather was nice and our trip through the islands was a smooth one. The two Chinese carpenters slept on the deck. The old man spent most of his time feeding and playing with his cats, which were given the run of the ship after we left port.

We set out course for Tao Atoll after I made my mail delivery to Puka-Puka. In all my years in the islands, I had only stopped at Tao twice—once just to take a look at a hexed island, and once to repair a damaged rudder. I don't think anyone else had visited it for years. It was the most useless piece of Pacific real estate I'd ever seen.

It was late evening when we tacked into the sheltered lagoon of the atoll and dropped anchor. I don't think the Cat Man slept a wink that night. He just sat on the cabin roof and gazed towards the beach. He certainly had a bad case of island fever. I couldn't help wondering if the old boy would find what it was he seemed to be looking for.

His damned cats were fascinated by the island, too. They squatted along the gunwales and fixed their shiny little eyes on the shore, their tails twitching expectantly. I would be glad to get rid of them. Cats always gave me the creeps.

I stayed anchored at Tao while Mr Foster got himself established. His carpenters built him a cosy little place with large screen windows. They made him bookcases for the hundreds of books he'd brought. They constructed a cistern to catch and store his water. supply. They even built him a small boat dock with the scraps of lumber left over.

While we worked, the six cats investigated their new home. In no time at all, each of them had caught and killed one of the scrawny, emaciated rats that infested the island. I hated rats even more than I did cats, so my attitude softened a little. Perhaps the old man was right; the cats might prove useful, after all.

The construction jobs completed, I prepared to leave the atoll. I made a deal with Mr Foster to stop at the island every three months on my mail run around the islands. I promised to keep him supplied with anything he needed. We both realized that I was going to be his only contact with the rest of the world.

We shook hands on the miniature dock when I was ready to shove off. Suddenly he snapped his fingers to indicate a sudden recollection.

"By the way, Captain, you'd better add a case of beef and a case of salmon to that order I gave you. It might come in handy for cat food."

This was too much! After years of living and dealing with people who considered any canned food an expensive luxury, I was understandably shocked.

"*Cat food?*"

The old man seemed amused at my lack of imagination. "Certainly," he said. "You don't expect the rats on this island to last forever, do you? I wouldn't want to see my little pets go hungry."

As usual, the little gent made sense. I had to admit there probably wouldn't be much left of the rodent population by the time I returned.

"O.K., Mister Foster," I agreed. "I'll bring your cat food. A pretty damned penny you're going to pay to feed these animals, but I guess you can spend your own money the way you want."

We parted amicably, and I manoeuvred the sloop out of the lagoon with the tide. I set course for the Marquesas Islands and took one last look at the Cat Man's low atoll before it sank below the horizon.

I worked the islands in a counter-clockwise direction, and averaged four complete trips a year. My home port was Papeete, the capital of the Societies. I covered my route around Tahiti first, then south along the Tubuais. I had four stops in the Tuamotus before I sailed north for the Marquesas and then completed my circular route back to Papeete. The whole trip usually consumed a day or two over two months, which left me plenty of time for a charter job between runs. The new stop at Tao would add three days to my regular journey, but I didn't mind. The Cat Man appeared to be loaded with money, and I could see he was going to be a darned good customer.

On my next stop at Tao, three months later, I saw the happiest man I'd ever remembered seeing. He was brown as a nut, and his face radiated health and good humour. If it weren't for his pile of white hair, he would have looked twenty years younger. Once again I had to admire him. He had come to the islands to find his private little Utopia, and he had found it!

The little fellow bubbled over with excitement as he went through the books and mail I delivered to him. He extracted a cheque from one envelope and endorsed it to me in payment for the supplies I had brought, and asked me to bring the balance of the money to him on my next trip. I was impressed at the amount of the cheque. I had never heard of him before, but apparently he made a good living with his typewriter.

I picked up his pile of finished manuscripts and promised to see that they were airmailed to New York. He ordered the usual supplies and doubled his previous order for cat food. Two of his females had litters of kittens. He showed them to me proudly, and I could see he got a lot of pleasure from their company. He'd been right about the rats, too. Hardly any were left on the once-infested island.

On my next stop, he had another stack of manuscripts for me, and more new kittens. They were certainly thriving on the atoll. The old man was thriving, too. I couldn't get over the fact that he was enjoying his self-imposed exile on that dreary little palm-tree prison, and my esteem for him continued to grow. I delivered a load of cash from his previous cheque, and he endorsed new ones to me. He put the money in a strong box he kept in his cabin. Again he doubled his order for cat food.

By the time three years had passed, that damned atoll was crawling with cats. I could hear them yowling at the sight of my sloop when I entered the lagoon: they knew I was carrying the commissary. Mr Foster met my dory while standing on his dock in a mob of cats. For the first time, I noticed a tight look about his features and a slight nervousness in his manner. I had an uneasy feeling that my miracle man was beginning to wear at the seams.

But his greeting was warmer than usual. "Good day, Captain Rogers. I certainly am glad to see you."

We had to practically kick our way through the cats to get to his cabin. The old man yelled at them and waved his cane threateningly. My curiosity got the better of me.

"Mister Foster," I asked, "how many cats do you think you have now?"

He answered with a noticeable lack of enthusiasm.

"Oh, I don't know—over a hundred, I guess."

"Well, at least you don't have to worry about the rats any more," I chuckled.

He turned to me with an amused smile. "Rats?" he asked. "I don't have to worry about anything any more. They've climbed the palms and cleaned out all the bird nests on the island. The birds won't come near the place now. They've caught and eaten just about every insect on the atoll. I ran out of food for them a week ago, and the little devils haven't given me a moment's peace. I finally had to stop writing and spend all my time fishing for them."

I could see the animals could be quite a problem if they were hungry. I was making a good profit on the cat food I was hauling him, but the situation appeared to be getting out of hand.

"Looks like you brought too many females in your original batch," I said. "Want me to take half of them with me when I leave, and drop them over the side?"

The Cat Man drew back in horror.

"Oh, heavens no!" he gasped. "I couldn't consider such a thing." Then his face brightened and his usual kind expression returned. He stooped and picked up a purring, half-grown kitten.

"My pets are really quite interesting, Captain Rogers. Of course, there are so many now, they've lost their individuality to me to some extent, but the feline society they have organized is fascinating."

He turned and pointed to the window. "See that ragged-eared big tom rubbing against the screen?"

I could see the mangy-looking beast. He looked as if he'd been in a thousand fights and lost every one of them.

"That one is the king of my tribe, and he has a goon squad of young toms who back him up. They have their pick of the females. And the care the mother cats give to their young ones is something wonderful to witness. I admit they're getting to be a problem, but life here would be pretty dull without them."

He didn't quite convince me this time.

I tried another angle. "At least let me try to round up a couple of natives who aren't too superstitious to come here and do your fishing for you. There's enough fish in that lagoon to feed a million cats."

The old man shook his white head vigorously.

"No, no, Captain. I came here to get away from people so I could write. I'll put up with a thousand cats before I'll share my solitude with anyone."

I didn't push the issue. It was his life, his world; he had made it for himself. I left him the supplies he'd ordered, and tossed in an extra case of beef from my own stores. It would take a lot of rations to feed a hundred cats for three months. I noted that the finished manuscripts he handed me were about half their usual bulk.

The story of the Cat Man and his pets had spread throughout French Oceania. By now, the rations I was hauling for his beasts were making up a large part of my load, and Tao Atoll was a subject of much amusement in Papeete. Several people, with apparently nothing else to do, were always waiting for me to return from my trip with news of the old man and his cats. He didn't realize it, but he was a famous man in the South Pacific, and not because of his writing, either.

On my next trip I found him beginning to crack. He'd run short of food again, and the cats were really starting to wear him down. I saw something else in his face that I'd never seen before. It was fear.

As usual, he met me standing on his dock, completely surrounded with a yowling pack of hungry cats.

"Did you bring the cat food, Captain Rogers?" he yelled over the din.

"Everything you ordered, sir," I answered, as I tossed him the rope from my dory.

Again, we had to kick our way through the cats to reach his cabin. The old man surely was mistaken in his last estimate of their population. It appeared to me there were closer to two hundred cats. On an island a mile long and a hundred yards wide, that's a lot of cats.

He started complaining about his pets as soon as we got into the cabin, ready to admit they were now a serious problem.

"These last two weeks have been a nightmare, Captain," he whined. "I started fishing a month ago, when it became obvious that their rations wouldn't last. I've never seen such voracious beasts."

His face was lined with worry. He had lost his neat, tidy appearance, and his face looked haunted. His island Utopia was rapidly turning into a hell. His dream was threatening to disintegrate before his eyes.

"I'm afraid we'll have to do something about the cats after all," he complained. "I have no manuscripts for you this time. These animals haven't given me any peace. Their mating screams and their begging voices! The toms have taken to eating the new-born kittens and the fights are practically continuous. I must do something!"

I wasn't surprised to hear him talk this way. I'd seen the initial signs of a crack-up on my last trip. The old man was beginning to recognize realities.

"Shall I bring you some poison for them on my next trip, Mister Foster?" I offered.

"Poison?" He flinched, as I knew he would. He closed his eyes and squeezed his forehead with nervous fingers. Then he opened his eyes and looked at me.

"No, definitely not," he said. "I could never be that cruel. Their being here is my own doing, and no fault of the cats. There must be some other solution."

I smiled and patted the old man on the shoulder. "I hope you'll forgive me, Mister Foster, but I anticipated your getting fed up with the cats. I brought along a couple of dogs for you this trip."

Now it was the Cat Man's turn to be surprised. "Dogs?" he exclaimed. Then a gleam of hope came into his eyes.

"That's right, Mister Foster. I thought maybe you could tie them up around your cabin. They'd keep the cats from bothering you."

He was pleased. His eyes grew brighter and the old smile returned to his face. He snatched my hand and wrung it gratefully. I was glad I'd brought them. If he hadn't consented to my leaving them, I planned to kick them overboard before I sailed anyhow, and let them swim to shore. I liked the little guy too much to see a mess of cats ruin his paradise.

"They're both males, too," I added as I turned to go after the dogs. "You won't have to worry about their breeding you out of your island."

The folks back in Papeete got a kick when I told them about the dogs. I had rounded up the meanest canines I could find in the Tuamotus. They didn't even like themselves, and they would both go wild at the sight of a cat. However, the way things turned out, I guess I wasn't as smart as I thought I was. Two dogs were a pretty poor match for two hundred hungry cats.

The cats had about taken over completely by the time I reached Tao on my next trip. I could hear them yowling as I entered the lagoon. I was listening for the barking of the dogs, but I never heard a yip.

I saw the old man's face peering at me from his screened window as I rowed the dory towards his dock. Just before I reached the dock, I heard his door slam. I looked up to see him scurrying towards me, and thrashing with his cane. The leaping, screaming cats made way for him, but they were bold as hell. They'd just jump out of range of the cane and stand there spitting at him with their backs arched.

Foster had to knock about a dozen of them into the water before he could grab my rope. We fought our way to his cabin. I noticed the dog chains and empty collars as I dashed through the doors. The screams of the hungry cats were deafening.

When I finally got my breath and faced the old man, I was shocked. I hope I never see a look like that on a human face again. His eyes were sunken, his skin stretched over his sharp cheek bones, and his lips drawn in a thin line against his yellowed teeth. He was filthy, and he obviously hadn't shaved for days.

He didn't have to tell me what he'd been through. The din of the cats tearing at the screens told the story. I would have dreaded the prospect of staying there a day, let alone weeks. The poor man had lived through a hell of his own making. I knew he wasn't completely mad yet, or he wouldn't have had the courage to meet me at the dock.

"The dogs!" I shouted. "Where are the dogs?"

The Cat Man was glaring at me like an idiot.

"They ate them," he said, in a strange metallic voice. "Two weeks ago. They killed and ate them—down to the last hair and toenail. The dogs killed a few of the cats and the cats ate their own corpses. They've been after me ever since."

In spite of his appearance, I could see the old man still had a good grip on himself. Best thing I could do was to get those cats fed before they ripped us both to pieces. I snatched up his cane and went for the door.

A couple of the beasts leaped on my back from the roof as I dashed for the dock. They gave me some nasty bites and scratches before I shook them off. I killed five with the cane before they learned my reach was longer than old Foster's. Each stricken cat was immediately eaten by his famished brothers and sisters.

I loaded the dory with cases of cat food from the sloop, and rowed to within twenty feet of the beach. For two hours I sat and tossed them open tins until my fingers were covered with blisters made by the can opener.

When the last cat had slunk away, gorged, I beached the dory and made my way back to the old man's cabin. He was sitting with his head on the table—asleep!

A couple of hours' rest, a bath, a shave, and some of the fear gone out of his face, and the little gent looked something like his old self.

We had coffee and got down to cases. I put it to him squarely.

"I don't suppose I can make you leave this place?"

He wagged his head, "Never, Captain."

I figured as much. Characters like Mr Foster have that dogged determination that moves mountains. Guess that's why I liked him.

"Well, then," I continued, "we're going to have to do something about the cats. I'm going to bring a load of poison next trip."

In spite of the horrifying experience he'd been through, the word "poison" still made him grimace. "Must it be poison, Captain?" he asked hopefully.

"Now don't try to talk me out of it," I warned. "I'm going to get rid of these cats if I have to tie you up to do it."

He agreed, reluctantly. "I suppose you're right. It seems impossible to control them, and I must get back to my writing."

I hated to leave him with the cats again, but I had no choice. I had brought even more cat food than he'd ordered, but it still wasn't enough. I raided my own stores and gave him all I could part with. I handed him my carbine on my last trip in the dory.

"Better take this, just in case," I urged him. He accepted it with the air of a person indulging another's whim. I fished a box of cartridges out of my pocket and tossed it to him.

"Careful with these and don't waste them," I warned. "There are only fifty rounds in that box, and that's all I have."

He accepted the box with a sad but grateful smile. As I pulled away from the dock, I yelled my last bit of advice.

"Aim at the toms!"

I should have shot fifty of the cats myself before I left. That way the rations would have gone a lot further. However, I had already decided to make a quick trip and return with the poison as soon as I could. Besides, I couldn't bear the thought of shooting them while the Cat Man was watching. He feared them, but he still couldn't stand to see them hurt.

I hurried through my business in Papeete, and was back at sea in three days. The hurricane caught me in the Tubuais. It wasn't the worst blow that ever hit the islands, but it was the worst that I'd been through. I weathered the storm on one of the atolls with the natives. My sloop snapped her moorings and was driven among the palms. It was almost a total wreck.

When the sea calmed down, I hired a native out-rigger to take me back to Papeete. It was a long, miserable trip, but we made it. I guess I had a foolish notion I could hire or buy another boat and go about my business, or at least get the old man's stuff to him at Tao. I hadn't realized how bad the hurricane had been until I saw Papeete.

The Society Islands had taken the full force of the storm, and the results were appalling. Ninety per cent of the boats and ships tied up were wrecked or damaged. You couldn't hire, buy, or steal a deep water boat. I forgot about my own misfortunes when I got a glimpse at the destruction in the harbour at Papeete. All I could think of was that poor old guy on that island with all those cats!

Not being able to get a boat, I had to do the next best thing. I bought bolts, caulking, sail cloth, and everything else that I thought the natives and I could carry on the out-rigger, and headed back to the Tubuais. I figured we could put my own sloop together again, at least good enough to get back to Cat Island.

Natives hate work and I just about killed those boys of mine with it. We took that pile of scrap lumber and began reassembling it. I drove them from dawn to dusk, relentlessly, and worked after dark by lantern light. What we needed and didn't have, we made. In six weeks we had the sloop in shape. I'll admit she wasn't very sound, but I knew she'd stand quite a bit of sailing if I kept her out of rough weather.

All the time we laboured I was spurred on by thoughts of the old man on Tao. He had rations for those hungry cats for only three months, and the morning we refloated the sloop made three months to the day since I had left him. Counting time I would lose going back to Papeete to replenish my supplies, it would take another month to get there.

Like the other white men in the islands, I never gave much thought to native taboos. They are based on cultural habits and legends rather than on factual data. However, a nervous uneasiness came over me twenty-six days later, when I was one day out of Tao. The sea was calm. The wind was light and steady and the sky was a clean, pale blue. Everything was normal for that time of the year, but I had a feeling I was leaving the world of the living and sailing towards the gates of hell.

I slipped into the lagoon just after midnight, and dropped anchor. Immediately a moan of sound rose from the black outline of the atoll and came across the moonlight-drenched mirror of water. My scalp rippled and I felt the skin tighten on the back of my neck. The starving beasts had heard me, and they were yowling for their rations.

I searched in vain for a light in the old man's shack. I gave him about a dozen yells across the lagoon, but was answered only by rising peaks in the continuous moaning of the cats. I searched for a sign of life from shore, and then I saw them. Cat eyes! Hundreds of them reflecting the light from the full moon, and glittering like silver sequins scattered on the black velvet shore of the atoll. They were still there, hungry and waiting. A wave of nausea swept over me as I realized I was too late. I wondered how many the old man had killed before they got him.

I waited for the sky to turn grey in the east before I unlimbered the dory. I didn't want to tackle that island until daylight. When the sun came up, I armed myself with two billy clubs, and started rowing towards the shore. When I approached the beach I saw a sight I'll remember the rest of my life. Several of the cats were splashing and diving in the shallow waters close to the shore, and swimming around like seals. They were fishing!

Two of the big toms swam out to meet my dory and tried to climb over the side. I brained them with the billy. I didn't try to make the dock. It was completely covered with the damned beasts and I was afraid they'd leap into the dory and swamp me when I tried to tie up. The beach was literally carpeted with cats. They were screaming at me in a maddening crescendo as though I were personally responsible for their plight. As I rowed down to the far end of the beach they followed me on the shore, an evil, mottled wave of spitting fur.

Again I opened tins of food to throw to them until my fingers were raw. When I emptied the dory I rowed back to the dock. About half of the cats followed me back and were waiting there to meet me. I vetoed the dock and shot the dory towards the beach with swift strokes. Just before she touched bottom, I shipped the oars, grabbed up my billy clubs, and got ready to jump.

I landed running, swinging my clubs like a windmill. I was killing cats with practically every swing, but they still tried to swarm over me. I yelled when I felt their teeth. The damned animals were insane. They were so crazy from hunger they would attack anything.

I literally beat my way to the old man's cabin, and very nearly didn't make it. The screens were torn as I knew they'd be. I didn't stop to open the door. I hit it with my shoulder and my momentum carried me through it with splinters flying. In a haze of pain and anger I saw the cats fighting over something in the centre of the floor. I knew that something had to be Mr Foster.

I went as crazy as the cats then. Ignoring the beasts that were clinging to my body, I began to beat a hole through that writhing pile of fur before me. The clubs rose and fell as I methodically smashed their bodies, until I could see what they were fighting over. It was a pile of snow-white hair attached to a bit of scalp.

I think I went completely out of my head. I don't know how I got out of that cabin, but I do know I must have been crazy to drop one of my clubs and grab up the old man's hair. I remember running for the beach with cats clinging all over me. I dived over the prow of the beached dory and smashed into it in a headlong swan dive.

That dive saved my life. The force of my body striking the stern unbeached the dory and sent it shooting out into the lagoon. I ripped the cats off me and knocked them silly with the remaining club.

I threw my shredded clothes away and doctored my hundreds of scratches and bites on the way back to Papeete. I made a full report to the French Governor, but I could tell he didn't believe me. Nevertheless, he sent a launch full of local police to investigate Tao a week later. When that launch got back, my stories about Cat Island sounded like Sunday School tales.

The police long boat didn't even make the beach at Tao. The

swimming cats met them in the lagoon. They climbed the oars and tried to eat the investigators on the spot. The police got out of there fast. They reported the cats had completely covered the atoll, and were fishing the lagoon like penguins. That's how its name "Cat Island" became official.

Everyone gives that atoll a wide berth now. No one has gone near it for years. I sail by it on my regular runs but I never stop. Sometimes I get to thinking about all that money the old man had in that strong box, and play with the idea of going back after it. When such a silly notion comes over me I just count my scars and dig out a little souvenir from my sea chest. Every time I look at old man Foster's hair I change my mind.

THE WHITE CAT OF DRUMGUNNIOL

by Joseph Sheridan Le Fanu

A RELATIVE OF *the playwright Richard Sheridan, Joseph Sheridan Le Fanu (1814–1873) abandoned law to take up journalism and eventually became proprietor and editor of several magazines including the* Dublin University Magazine *to which he contributed numerous short stories of terror and the supernatural. In addition, between 1845 and 1873 he wrote fourteen novels, the best known being* The House by the Churchyard, Checkmate *and* Uncle Silas—*a masterpiece of brooding evil. Among his many remarkable short stories is the Vampire tale,* Carmilla, *which has frequently been adapted for the screen, the most recent production being* The Vampire Lovers.

Towards the end of his life, Le Fanu's preoccupation with the macabre and morbid made him shun human company more and more. M. R. James, who was no poor judge, considered him to have been Britain's finest writer of ghostly tales.

There is a famous story of a white cat, with which we all become acquainted in the nursery. I am going to tell a story of a white cat very different from the amiable and enchanted princess who took that disguise for a season. The white cat of which I speak was a more sinister animal.

The traveller from Limerick towards Dublin, after passing the hills of Killaloe upon the left, as Keeper Mountain rises high in view, finds himself gradually hemmed in, up the right, by a range of lower hills. An undulating plain that dips gradually to a lower level than that of the road interposes, and some scattered hedgerows relieve its somewhat wild and melancholy character.

One of the few human habitations that send up their films of turf-smoke from that lonely plain, is the loosely thatched, earth-built dwelling of a "strong farmer", as the more prosperous of the tenant-farming classes are termed in Munster. It stands in a clump of trees near the edge of a wandering stream, about half-way between the mountains and the Dublin road, and had been for generations tenanted by people named Donovan.

In a distant place, desirous of studying some Irish records which had fallen into my hands, and inquiring for a teacher capable of instructing me in the Irish language, a Mr Donovan, dreamy, harmless, and learned, was recommended to me for the purpose.

I found that he had been educated as a Sizar in Trinity College, Dublin. He now supported himself by teaching, and the special direction of my studies, I suppose, flattered his national partialities, for he unbosomed himself of much of his long-reserved thoughts, and recollections about his country and his early days. It was he who told me this story, and I mean to repeat it, as nearly as I can, in his own words.

I have myself seen the old farmhouse, with its orchard of huge moss-grown apple trees. I have looked round on the peculiar landscape; the roofless, ivied tower, that two hundred years before had afforded a refuge from raid and rapparee, and which still occupies its old place in the angle of the haggard; the bush-grown "liss", that scarcely a hundred and fifty steps away records the labours of a bygone race; the dark and towering outline of old Keeper in the background; and the lonely range of furze and heath-clad hills that form a nearer barrier, with many a line of grey rock and clump of dwarf oak or birch. The pervading sense of loneliness made it a scene not unsuited for a wild and unearthly story. And I could quite fancy how, seen in the grey of a wintry morning, shrouded far and wide in snow, or in the melancholy glory of an autumnal sunset, or in the chill splendour of a moonlight night, it might have helped to tone a dreamy mind like honest Dan Donovan's to superstition and a proneness to the illusion of fancy. It is certain, however, that I never anywhere met with a more simple-minded creature, or one on whose good faith I could more entirely rely.

When I was a boy, said he, living at home at Drumgunniol, I

used to take my Goldsmith's *Roman History* in my hand and go down to my favourite seat, the flat stone, sheltered by a hawthorn tree beside the little lough, a large and deep pool, such as I have heard called a tarn in England. It lay in the gentle hollow of a field that is overhung towards the north by the old orchard, and being a deserted place was favourable to my studious quietude.

One day reading here, as usual, I wearied at last, and began to look about me, thinking of the heroic scenes I had just been reading of. I was as wide awake as I am at this moment, and I saw a woman appear at the corner of the orchard and walk down the slope. She wore a long, light grey dress, so long that it seemed to sweep the grass behind her, and so singular was her appearance in a part of the world where female attire is so inflexibly fixed by custom, that I could not take my eyes off her. Her course lay diagonally from corner to corner of the field, which was a large one, and she pursued it without swerving.

When she came near I could see that her feet were bare, and that she seemed to be looking steadfastly upon some remote object for guidance. Her route would have crossed me—had the tarn not interposed—about ten or twelve yards below the point at which I was sitting. But instead of arresting her course at the margin of the lough, as I had expected, she went on without seeming conscious of its existence, and I saw her, as plainly as I see you, sir, walk across the surface of the water, and pass, without seeming to see me, at about the distance I had calculated.

I was ready to faint from sheer terror. I was only thirteen years old then, and I remember every particular as if it had happened this hour.

The figure passed through the gap at the far corner of the field, and there I lost sight of it. I had hardly strength to walk home, and was so nervous, and ultimately so ill, that for three weeks I was confined to the house, and could not bear to be alone for a moment. I never entered that field again such was the horror with which from that moment every object in it was clothed. Even at this distance of time I should not like to pass through it.

This apparition I connected with a mysterious event; and, also, with a singular liability, that has for nearly eighty years distinguished, or rather afflicted, our family. It is no fancy. Everybody in that part of the country knows all about it. Everybody connected what I had seen with it.

I will tell it all to you as well as I can.

When I was about fourteen years old—that is about a year after the sight I had seen in the lough field—we were one night expecting my father home from the fair of Killoloe. My mother sat up to welcome him home, and I was with her, for I liked nothing better than such a vigil. My brothers and sisters, and the farm servants, except the men who were driving home the cattle from the fair, were asleep in their beds. My mother and I were sitting in the chimney corner chatting together, and watching my father's supper, which was kept hot over the fire. We knew that he would return before the men who were driving home the cattle, for he was riding, and told us that he would only wait to see them fairly on the road, and then push homeward.

At length we heard his voice and the knocking of his loaded whip at the door, and my mother let him in. I don't think I ever saw my father drunk, which is more than most men of my age, from the same part of the country, could say of theirs. But he could drink his glass of whiskey as well as another, and he usually came home from fair or market a little merry and mellow, and with a jolly flush in his cheeks.

Tonight he looked sunken, pale, and sad. He entered with the saddle and bridle in his hand, and he dropped them against the wall, near the door, and put his arms round his wife's neck, and kissed her kindly.

"Welcome home, Meehal," said she, kissing him heartily.

"God bless you, mavourneen," he answered.

And hugging her again, he turned to me, who was plucking him by the hand, jealous of his notice. I was little, and light of my age, and he lifted me up in his arms, and kissed me, and my arms being about his neck, he said to my mother:

"Draw the bolt, acuishla."

She did so, and setting me down very dejectedly, he walked to the fire and sat down on a stool, and stretched his feet towards the glowing turf, leaning with his hands on his knees.

"Rouse up, Mick, darlin'," said my mother, who was growing anxious, "and tell me how did the cattle sell, and did everything go lucky at the fair, or is there anything wrong with the landlord, or what in the world is it that ails you, Mick, jewel?"

"Nothin', Molly. The cows sould well, thank God, and there's nothin' fell out between me an' the landlord, an' everything's the same way. There's no fault to find anywhere."

"Well, then, Mickey, since so it is, turn round to your hot supper, and ate it, and tell us is there anything new."

"I got my supper, Molly, on the way, and I can't ate a bit," he answered.

"Got your supper on the way, an' you knowin' 'twas waiting for you at home, an' your wife sittin' up an' all!" cried my mother, reproachfully.

"You're takin' a wrong meanin' out of what I say," said my father. "There's something happened that leaves me that I can't eat a mouthful, and I'll not be dark with you, Molly, for, maybe, it ain't very long I have to be here, an' I'll tell you what it was. It's what I've seen, the white cat."

"The Lord between us and harm!" exclaimed my mother, in a moment as pale and as chap-fallen as my father; and then, trying to rally, with a laugh, she said: "Ha! 'tis only funnin' me you are. Sure a white rabbit was snared a Sunday last, in Grady's wood; an' Teigue seen a big white rat in the haggard yesterday."

" 'Twas neither rat nor rabbit was in it. Don't ye think but I'd know a rat or a rabbit from a big white cat, with green eyes as big as halfpennies, and its back riz up like a bridge, trottin' on and across me, and ready, if I dar' stop, to rub its sides against my shins and maybe to make a jump and seize my throat, if that it's a cat at all, an' not something worse?"

As he ended his description in a low tone, looking straight at the fire my father drew his big hand across his forehead once or twice, his face being damp and shining with the moisture of fear, and he sighed, or rather groaned, heavily.

My mother had relapsed into panic, and was praying again in her fear. I, too, was terribly frightened, and on the point of crying, for I knew all about the white cat.

Clapping my father on the shoulder, by way of encouragement, my mother leaned over him, kissing him, and at last began to cry. He was wringing her hands in his, and seemed in great trouble.

"There was nothin' came into the house with me?" he asked, in a very low tone, turning to me.

"There was nothin', father," I said, "but the saddle and bridle that was in your hand."

"Nothin' white kem in at the doore wid me," he repeated.

"Nothin' at all," I answered.

"So best," said my father, and making the sign of the cross, he began mumbling to himself, and I knew he was saying his prayers.

Waiting for a while, to give him time for this exercise, my mother asked him where he first saw it.

"When I was riding up the bohereen"—the Irish term meaning a little road, such as leads up to a farmhouse—"I bethought myself that the men was on the road with the cattle, and no one to look to the horse barrin' myself, so I thought I might as well leave him in the crooked field below, an' I tuck him there, he bein' cool, and not a hair turned, for I rode him aisy all the way. It was when I turned, after lettin' him go—the saddle and bridle bein' in my hand—that I saw it, pushin' out o' the long grass at the side o' the path, an' it walked across it, in front of me, an' then back again, before me, the same way, an' sometimes at one side, an' then at the other, lookin' at me wid them shinin' eyes; and I consayted I heard it growlin' as it kep' beside me—as close as ever you see—till I kem up to the doore, here, an' knocked an' called, as ye heered me."

Now, what was it, in so simple an incident, that agitated my father, my mother, myself, and finally, every member of this rustic household, with a terrible foreboding? It was this that we, one and all, believed that my father had received, in thus encountering the white cat, a warning of his approaching death.

The omen had never failed hitherto. It did not fail now. In a week after my father took the fever that was going, and before a month he was dead.

My honest friend, Dan Donovan, paused here; I could perceive that he was praying, for his lips were busy, and I concluded that it was for the repose of that departed soul.

In a little while he resumed.

It is eighty years now since that omen first attached to my family. Eighty years? Ay, is it. Ninety is nearer the mark. And I have spoken to many old people, in those earlier times, who had a distinct recollection of everything connected with it.

It happened in this way.

My grand-uncle, Connor Donovan, had the old farm of Drumgunniol in his day. He was richer than ever my father was, or my father's father either, for he took a short lease of Balraghan, and made money out of it. But money won't soften a hard heart, and I'm afraid my grand-uncle was a cruel man—a profligate man he was, surely, and that is mostly a cruel man at heart. He drank his share, too, and cursed and swore, when he was vexed, more than was good for his soul, I'm afraid.

At that time there was a beautiful girl of the Colemans, up in the mountains, not far from Capper Cullen. I'm told that there are no Colemans there now at all, and that family has passed away. The famine years made great changes.

Ellen Coleman was her name. The Colemans were not rich. But, being such a beauty, she might have made a good match. Worse than she did for herself, poor thing, she could not.

Con Donovan—my grand-uncle, God forgive him!—sometimes in his rambles saw her at fairs or patterns, and he fell in love with her, as who might not?

He used her ill. He promised her marriage, and persuaded her to come away with him; and, after all, he broke his word. It was just the old story. He tired of her, and he wanted to push himself in the world; and he married a girl of the Collopys, that had a great fortune—twenty-four cows, seventy sheep, and a hundred and twenty goats.

He married this Mary Collopy, and grew richer than before; and Ellen Coleman died broken-hearted. But that did not trouble the strong farmer much.

He would have liked to have children, but he had none, and this was the only cross he had to bear, for everything else went much as he wished.

One night he was returning from the fair of Nenagh. A shallow stream at that time crossed the road—they have thrown a bridge over it, I am told, some time since—and its channel was often dry in summer weather. When it was so, as it passes close by the old farmhouse of Drumgunniol, without a great deal of winding, it makes a sort of road, which people then used as a short cut to reach the house by. Into this dry channel, as there was plenty of light from the moon, my grand-uncle turned his horse, and when he had reached the two ash trees at the meering of the farm he turned his horse short into the river field, intending to ride through the gap at the other end, under the oak tree, and so he would have been within a few hundred yards of his door.

As he approached the "gap" he saw, or thought he saw, with a slow motion, gliding along the ground towards the same point, and now and then with a soft bound, a white object, which he described as being no bigger than his hat, but what it was he could not see, as it moved along the hedge and disappeared at the point to which he was himself tending.

When he reached the gap the horse stopped short. He urged and coaxed it in vain. He got down to lead it through, but it recoiled, snorted, and fell into a wild trembling fit. He mounted it again. But its terror continued, and it obstinately resisted his caresses and his whip. It was bright moonlight, and my grand-uncle was chafed by the horse's resistance, and, seeing nothing to account for it, and being so near home, what little patience he possessed forsook him, and, plying his whip and spur in earnest, he broke into oaths and curses.

All of a sudden the horse sprang through, and Con Donovan, as he passed under the broad branch of the oak, saw clearly a woman standing on the bank beside him, her arm extended, with the hand of which, as he flew by, she struck him a blow upon the shoulders. It threw him forward upon the neck of the horse, which, in wild terror, reached the door at a gallop, and stood there quivering and steaming all over.

Less alive than dead, my grand-uncle got in. He told his story, at least, so much as he chose. His wife did not quite know what to think. But that something very bad had happened she could not doubt. He was very faint and ill, and begged that the priest should be sent for forthwith. When they were getting him to his bed they saw distinctly the marks of five fingerprints on the flesh of his shoulder, where the spectral blow had fallen. These singular marks —which they said resembled in tint the hue of a body struck by lightning—remained imprinted on his flesh, and were buried with him.

When he had recovered sufficiently to talk with the people about him—speaking, like a man at his last hour, from a burdened heart, and troubled conscience—he repeated his story, but said he did not see, or, at all events, know, the face of the figure that stood in the gap. No one believed him. He told more about it to the priest than to others. He certainly had a secret to tell. He might as well have divulged it frankly, for the neighbours all knew well enough that it was the face of dead Ellen Coleman that he had seen.

From that moment my grand-uncle never raised his head. He was a scared, silent, broken-spirited man. It was early summer then, and at the fall of the leaf in the same year he died.

Of course there was a wake, such as beseemed a strong farmer so rich as he. For some reason the arrangements of this ceremonial were a little different from the usual routine.

The usual practice is to place the body in the great room, or kitchen, as it is called, of the house. In this particular case there was as I told you, for some reason, an unusual arrangement. The body was placed in a small room that opened upon the greater one. The door of this, during the wake, stood open. There were candles about the bed, and pipes and tobacco on the table, and stools for such guests as chose to enter, the door standing open for their reception.

The body, having been laid out, was left alone, in this smaller room, during the preparations for the wake. After nightfall one of the women, approaching the bed to get a chair which she had left near it, rushed from the room with a scream, and, having recovered her speech at the farther end of the "kitchen", and surrounded by a gaping audience, she said, at last:

"May I never sin, if his face bain't riz up again the back o' the bed, and he starin' down to the doore, wid eyes as big as pewter plates, that id be shinin' in the moon!"

"Arra, woman! Is it cracked you are?" said one of the farm boys as they are termed, being men of any age you please.

"Ahg, Molly, don't be talkin', woman! 'Tis what ye consayted it, goin' into the dark room, out o' the light. Why didn't ye take a candle in your fingers, ye aumadhaun?" said one of her female companions.

"Candle, or no candle; I seen it," insisted Molly. "An' what's more, I could a'most tak' my oath I seen his arum, too, stretchin' out o' the bed along the flure, three times as long as it should be, to take hould o' me be the fut.'

"Nansinse, ye fool, what id he want o' yer fut?" exclaimed one scornfully.

"Gi' me the candle, some o' yez—in the name o' God," said old Sal Doolan, that was straight and lean, and a woman that could pray like a priest almost.

"Give her a candle," agreed all.

But whatever they might say, there wasn't one among them that did not look pale and stern enough as they followed Mrs Doolan, who was praying as fast as her lips could patter, and leading the van with a tallow candle, held like a taper, in her fingers.

The door was half open, as the panic-stricken girl had left it; and holding the candle on high the better to examine the room, she made a step or so into it.

If my grand-uncle's hand had been stretched along the floor, in the unnatural way described, he had drawn it back again under the sheet that covered him. And tall Mrs Doolan was in no danger of tripping over his arm as she entered. But she had not gone more than a step or two with her candle aloft, when, with a drowning face, she suddenly stopped short, staring at the bed which was now fully in view.

"Lord, bless us, Mrs Doolan, ma'am, come back," said the woman next her, who had fast hold of her dress, or her "coat", as they call it, and drawing her backward with a frightened pluck, while a general recoil among her followers betokened the alarm which her hesitation had inspired.

"Whisht, will yez?" said the leader, peremptorily, "I can't hear my own ears wid the noise ye're makin', an' which iv yez let the cat here, an' whose cat is it?" she asked, peering suspiciously at a white cat that was sitting on the breast of the corpse.

"Put it away, will yez?" she resumed, with horror at the profanation. "Many a corpse as I sthretched and crossed in the bed, the likes o' that I never seen yet. The man o' the house, wid a brute baste like that mounted on him, like a phooka, Lord forgi' me for namin' the like in this room. Dhrive it away, some o' yez! out o' that, this minute, I tell ye."

Each repeated the order, but no one seemed inclined to execute it. They were crossing themselves, and whispering their conjectures and misgivings as to the nature of the beast, which was no cat of that house, nor one that they had ever seen before. On a sudden, the white cat placed itself on the pillow over the head of the body, and having from that place glared for a time at them over the features of the corpse, it crept softly along the body towards them, growling low and fiercely as it drew near.

Out of the room they bounced, in dreadful confusion, shutting the door fast after them, and not for a good while did the hardiest venture to peep in again.

The white cat was sitting in its old place, on the dead man's breast, but this time it crept quietly down the side of the bed, and disappeared under it, the sheet which was spread like a coverlet, and hung down nearly to the floor, concealed it from view.

Praying, crossing themselves, and not forgetting a sprinkling of holy water, they peeped, and finally searched, poking spades, "wattles", pitchforks and such implements under the bed. But the cat was not to be found, and they concluded that it had made its escape among their feet as they stood near the threshold. So they secured the door carefully, with hasp and padlock.

But when the door was opened next morning they found the white cat sitting, as if it had never been disturbed, upon the breast of the dead man.

Again occurred very nearly the same scene with a like result, only that some said they saw the cat afterwards lurking under a big box in a corner of the outer room, where my grand-uncle kept his leases and papers, and his prayer-book and beads.

Mrs Doolan heard it growling at her heels wherever she went; and although she could not see it, she could hear it spring on the back of her chair when she sat down, and growl in her ear, so that she would bounce up with a scream and a prayer, fancying that it was on the point of taking her by the throat.

And the priest's boy, looking round the corner, under the branches of the old orchard, saw a white cat sitting under the little window of the room where my grand-uncle was laid out and looking up at the four small panes of glass as a cat will watch a bird.

The end of it was that the cat was found on the corpse again, when the room was visited, and do what they might, whenever the body was left alone, the cat was found again in the same ill-omened contiguity with the dead man. And this continued, to the scandal and fear of the neighbourhood, until the door was opened finally for the wake.

My grand-uncle being dead, and, with all due solemnities, buried, I have done with him. But not quite yet with the white cat. No banshee ever yet was more inalienably attached to a family than this apparition is to mine. But there is this difference. The banshee seems to be animated with an affectionate sympathy with the bereaved family to whom it is hereditarily attached, whereas this thing has about it a suspicion of malice. It is the messenger simply of death. And its taking the shape of a cat—the coldest, and they say, the most vindictive of brutes—is indicative of the spirit of its visit.

When my grandfather's death was near, although he seemed quite well at the time, it appeared not exactly, but very nearly in the same way in which I told you it showed itself to my father.

The day before my Uncle Teigue was killed by the bursting of his gun, it appeared to him in the evening, at twilight, by the lough, in the field where I saw the woman who walked across the water, as I told you. My uncle was washing the barrel of his gun in the lough. The grass is short there, and there is no cover near it. He did not know how it approached but the first he saw of it, the white cat was walking close round his feet, in the twilight, with an angry twist of its tail, and a green glare in its eyes, and do what he would, it continued walking round and round him, in larger or smaller circles, till he reached the orchard, and there he lost it.

My poor Aunt Peg—she married one of the O'Brians, near Oolah —came to Drumgunniol to go to the funeral of a cousin who died about a mile away. She died herself, poor woman, only a month after.

Coming from the wake, at two or three o'clock in the morning, as she got over the stile into the farm of Drumgunniol, she saw the white cat at her side, and it kept close beside her, she ready to faint all the time, till she reached the door of the house, where it made a spring up into the white-thorn tree that grows close by, and so it parted from her. And my little brother Jim saw it also, just three weeks before he died. Every member of our family who dies, or takes his death-sickness, at Drumgunniol, is sure to see the white cat, and no one of us who sees it need hope for long life after.

ANCIENT SORCERIES

by Algernon Blackwood

ALGERNON BLACKWOOD (1869–1951) *wrote an impressive number of books including* The Empty House, The Listener, Day and Night Stories, Ten-Minute Stories, The Dance of Death, The Centaur *and many others—all the more impressive because he did not start his writing career until he was thirty-six.*

Initially, the young Blackwood left the restricting, Bible-thumping atmosphere of his Kentish home to seek his future in Canada. There, several business ventures proved unsuccessful and he fell upon hard times, drifting aimlessly around the North American continent before finally taking a job as a reporter on a New York newspaper. It was not until later when he returned to England that Blackwood began to write fiction other than purely for his own pleasure. He then chilled readers with a long succession of powerfully atmospheric tales of haunting and horror. Probably his finest creation in this genre was the occult investigator Dr John Silence who appears in several stories including Ancient Sorceries. *Later in life, Blackwood achieved considerable fame through his readings of ghost stories on BBC radio, earning himself the title of the "Ghost-man".*

Since youth Algernon Blackwood was deeply interested in the supernatural and believed strongly that the "Man in the Street possesses strange powers which never manifest themselves normally."

This beautiful story demonstrates that belief. It is also probably the best Cat story ever written, every page permeated with feline stealth and menace.

I

There are, it would appear, certain wholly unremarkable persons, with none of the characteristics that invite adventure, who yet once or twice in the course of their smooth lives undergo an experience so strange that the world catches its breath—and looks the other way! And it was cases of this kind, perhaps, more than any other, that fell into the widespread net of John Silence, the psychic doctor, and, appealing to his deep humanity, to his patience, and to his great qualities of spiritual sympathy, led often to the revelation of problems of the strangest complexity, and of the profoundest possible human interest.

Matters that seemed almost too curious and fantastic for belief he loved to trace to their hidden sources. To unravel a tangle in the very soul of things—and to release a suffering human soul in the process—was with him a veritable passion. And the knots he untied were, indeed, often passing strange.

The world, of course, asks for some plausible basis to which it can attach credence—something it can, at least, pretend to explain. The adventurous type it can understand: such people carry about with them an adequate explanation of their exciting lives, and their characters obviously drive them into the circumstances which produce the adventures. It expects nothing else from them, and is satisfied. But dull, ordinary folk have no right to out-of-the-way experiences, and the world having been led to expect otherwise, is disappointed with them, not to say shocked. Its complacent judgment has been rudely disturbed.

"Such a thing happen to *that* man!" it cries—"a commonplace person like that! It is too absurd! There must be something wrong!"

Yet there could be no question that something did actually happen to little Arthur Vezin, something of the curious nature he described to Dr Silence. Outwardly or inwardly, it happened beyond a doubt, and in spite of the jeers of his few friends who heard the tale, and observed wisely that "such a thing might perhaps have come to Iszard, that crack-brained Iszard, or to that odd fish Minski, but it could never have happened to commonplace little

Vezin, who was fore-ordained to live and die according to scale".

But, whatever his method of death was, Vezin certainly did not "live according to scale" so far as this particular event in his otherwise uneventful life was concerned; and to hear him recount it, and watch his pale features change, and hear his voice grow softer and more hushed as he proceeded, was to know the conviction that his halting words perhaps failed sometimes to convey. He lived the thing over again each time he told it. His whole personality became muffled in the recital. It subdued him more than ever, so that the tale became a lengthy apology for an experience that he deprecated. He appeared to excuse himself and ask your pardon for having dared to take part in so fantastic an episode. For little Vezin was a timid, gentle, sensitive soul, rarely able to assert himself, tender to man and beast, and almost constitutionally unable to say No, or to claim many things that should rightly have been his. His whole scheme of life seemed utterly remote from anything more exciting than missing a train or losing an umbrella or an omnibus. And when this curious event came upon him he was already more years beyond forty than his friends suspected or he cared to admit.

John Silence, who heard him speak of his experience more than once, said that he sometimes left out certain details and put in others; yet they were all obviously true. The whole scene was unforgettably cinematographed on to his mind. None of the details were imagined or invented. And when he told the story with them all complete, the effect was undeniable. His appealing brown eyes shone, and much of the charming personality, usually so carefully repressed, came forward and revealed itself. His modesty was always there, of course, but in the telling he forgot the present and allowed himself to appear almost vividly as he lived again in the past of his adventure.

He was on the way home when it happened, crossing northern France from some mountain trip or other where he buried himself solitarywise every summer. He had nothing but an unregistered bag in the rack, and the train was jammed to suffocation, most of the passengers being unredeemed holiday English. He disliked them, not because they were his fellow-countrymen, but because they were noisy and obtrusive, obliterating with their big limbs and tweed clothing all the quieter tints of the day that brought him satisfaction and enabled him to melt into insignificance and forget that he was anybody. These English clashed about him like a brass band, making him feel vaguely that he ought to be more self-assertive and obstreperous, and that he did not claim insistently enough all kinds of things that he didn't want and that were really valueless, such as corner seats, windows up or down and so forth.

So that he felt uncomfortable in the train, and wished the journey were over and he was back again living with his unmarried sister in Surbiton.

And when the train stopped for ten panting minutes at the little station in northern France, and he got out to stretch his legs on the platform, and saw to his dismay a further batch of the British Isles debouching from another train it suddenly seemed impossible to him to continue the journey. Even *his* flabby soul revolted, and the idea of staying a night in the little town and going on next day by a slower, emptier train, flashed into his mind. The guard was already shouting *"En voiture"*, and the corridor of his compartment was already packed, when the thought came to him. And, for once, he acted with decision and rushed to snatch his bag.

Finding the corridor and steps impassable, he tapped at the window (for he had a corner seat) and begged the Frenchman who sat opposite to hand his luggage out to him, explaining in his wretched French that he intended to break the journey there. And this elderly Frenchman, he declared, gave him a look, half of warning, half of reproach, that to his dying day he could never forget; handed the bag through the window of the moving train; and at the same time poured into his ears a long sentence, spoken rapidly and low, of which he was able to comprehend only the last few words: *"à cause du sommeil et à cause des chats"*.

In reply to Dr Silence, whose singular psychic acuteness at once seized upon this Frenchman as a vital point in the adventure, Vezin admitted that the man had impressed him favourably from the beginning, though without being able to explain why. They had sat facing one another during the four hours of the journey, and though no conversation had passed between them—Vezin was timid about his stuttering French—he confessed that his eyes were being continually drawn to his face, almost, he felt, to rudeness, and that each, by a dozen nameless little politenesses and attentions, had evinced the desire to be kind. The men liked each other and their personalities did not clash, or would not have clashed had they chanced to come to terms of acquaintance. The Frenchman, indeed, seemed to have exercised a silent protective influence over the insignificant little Englishman, and without words or gestures betrayed that he wished him well and would gladly have been of service to him.

"And this sentence that he hurled at you after the bag?" asked John Silence, smiling that peculiarly sympathetic smile that always melted the prejudices of his patient, "were you unable to follow it exactly?"

"It was so quick and low and vehement," explained Vezin, in his small voice, "that I missed practically the whole of it. I only caught the few words at the very end, because he spoke them so clearly, and his face was bent down out of the carriage window so near to mine."

"'*À cause du sommeil et à cause des chats*'?" repeated Dr Silence as though half speaking to himself.

"That's it, exactly," said Vezin; "which, I take it, means something like 'because of sleep and because of the cats,' doesn't it?"

"Certainly, that's how I should translate it," the doctor observed shortly, evidently not wishing to interrupt more than necessary.

"And the rest of the sentence—all the first part I couldn't understand, I mean—was a warning not to do something—not to stop in the town, or at some particular place in the town, perhaps. That was the impression it made on me."

Then, of course, the train rushed off, and left Vezin standing on the platform alone and rather forlorn.

The little town climbed in straggling fashion up a sharp hill rising out of the plain at the back of the station, and was crowned by the twin towers of the ruined cathedral peeping over the summit. From the station itself it looked uninteresting and modern, but the fact was that the medieval position lay out of sight just beyond the crest. And once he reached the top and entered the old streets, he stepped clean out of modern life into a bygone century. The noise and bustle of the crowded train seemed days away. The spirit of this silent hill-town, remote from tourists and motor-cars, dreaming its own quiet life under the autumn sun, rose up and cast its spell upon him. Long before he recognized this spell he acted under it. He walked softly, almost on tiptoe, down the winding narrow streets where the gables all but met over his head, and he entered the doorway of the solitary inn with a deprecating and modest demeanour that was in itself an apology for intruding upon the place and disturbing its dream.

At first, however, Vezin said, he noticed very little of all this. The attempt at analysis came much later. What struck him then was only the delightful contrast of the silence and peace after the dust and noisy rattle of the train. He felt soothed and stroked like a cat.

"Like a cat, you said?" interrupted John Silence, quickly catching him up.

"Yes. At the very start I felt that." He laughed apologetically. "I felt as though the warmth and the stillness and the comfort made me purr. It seemed to be the general mood of the whole place—then."

The inn, a rambling, ancient house, the atmosphere of the old coaching days still about it, apparently did not welcome him too warmly. He felt he was only tolerated, he said. But it was cheap and comfortable, and the delicious cup of afternoon tea he ordered at once made him feel really very pleased with himself for leaving the train in this bold, original way. For to him it had seemed bold and original. He felt something of a dog. His room, too, soothed him with its dark panelling and low, irregular ceiling, and the long, sloping passage that led to it seemed the natural pathway to a real Chamber of Sleep—a little, dim, cubby-hole out of the world where noise could not enter. It looked upon the court-yard at the back. It was all very charming, and made him think of himself as dressed in very soft velvet somehow, and the floors seemed padded, the walls provided with cushions. The sound of the streets could not penetrate there. It was an atmosphere of absolute rest that surrounded him.

On engaging the two-franc room he had interviewed the only person who seemed to be about that sleepy afternoon, an elderly waiter with Dundreary whiskers and a drowsy courtesy, who had ambled lazily towards him across the stone yard; but on coming downstairs again for a little promenade in the town before dinner he encountered the proprietress herself. She was a large woman whose hands, feet, and features seemed to swim towards him out of a sea of person. They merged, so to speak. But she had great, dark, vivacious eyes that counteracted the bulk of her body and betrayed the fact that in reality she was both vigorous and alert. When he first caught sight of her she was knitting in a low chair against the sunlight of the wall, and something at once made him see her as a great tabby cat, dozing, yet awake, heavily sleepy, and yet at the same time prepared for instantaneous action. A great mouser on the watch occurred to him.

She took him in with a single, comprehensive glance that was polite without being cordial. Her neck, he noticed, was extraordinarily supple in spite of its proportions, for it turned so easily to follow him, and the head it carried bowed so very flexibly.

"But when she looked at me, you know," said Vezin, with that little, apologetic smile in his brown eyes, and that faintly deprecating gesture of the shoulders that was characteristic of him, "the odd notion came to me that really she had intended to make quite a different movement, and that with a single bound she could have leaped at me across the width of that stone yard and pounced upon me like some huge cat upon a mouse."

He laughed a little soft laugh, and Dr Silence made a note in his book without interrupting, while Vezin proceeded in a tone as though he feared he had already told too much, and more than we could believe.

"Very soft, yet very active she was, for all her size and mass, and I felt she knew what I was doing even after I had passed and was behind her back. She spoke to me, and her voice was smooth and running. She asked if I had my luggage, and was comfortable in my room, and then added that dinner was at seven o'clock, and that they were very early people in this little country town. Clearly, she intended to convey that late hours were not encouraged."

Evidently, she contrived by voice and manner to give him the impression that here he would be "managed", that everything would be arranged and planned for him, and that he had nothing to do but fall into the groove and obey. No decided action or sharp personal effort would be looked for from him. It was the very reverse of the train. He walked quietly out into the street, feeling soothed and peaceful. He realized that he was in a *milieu* that suited him and stroked him the right way. It was so much easier to be obedient. He began to purr again, and to feel that all the town purred with him.

About the streets of that little town he meandered gently, falling deeper and deeper into the spirit of repose that characterized it. With no special aim he wandered up and down, to and fro. The September sunshine fell slantingly over the roofs. Down winding alleyways, fringed with tumbling gables and open casements, he caught fairylike glimpses of the great plain below, and of the meadows and yellow copses lying like a dream-map in the haze. The spell of the past held very potently here, he felt.

The streets were full of picturesquely garbed men and women, all busy enough, going their respective ways; but no one took any notice of him or turned to stare at his obviously English appearance. He was even able to forget that with his tourist appearance he was a false note in a charming picture, and he melted more and more into the scene, feeling delightfully insignificant and unimportant and unself-conscious. It was like becoming part of a softly coloured dream which he did not even realize to be a dream.

On the eastern side the hill fell away more sharply, and the plain below ran off rather suddenly into a sea of gathering shadows in which the little patches of woodland looked like islands and the stubble fields like deep water. Here he strolled along the old ramparts of ancient fortifications that once had been formidable, but now were only vision-like with their charming mingling of broken, grey walls and wayward vine and ivy. From the broad coping on which he sat for a moment, level with the rounded tops of clipped plane-trees, he saw the esplanade far below lying in shadow. Here and there a yellow sunbeam crept in and lay upon the fallen yellow leaves, and from the height he looked down and saw the townsfolk were walking to and fro in the cool of the evening. He could just hear the sound of their slow footfalls, and the murmur of their voices floated up to him through the gaps between the trees. The figures looked like shadows as he caught glimpses of their quiet movements far below.

He sat there for some time pondering, bathed in the waves of murmurs and half-lost echoes that rose to his ears, muffled by the leaves of the plane-trees. The whole town, and the little hill out of which it grew as naturally as an ancient wood, seemed to him like a being lying there half asleep on the plain and crooning to itself as it dozed.

And, presently, as he sat lazily melting into its dream, a sound of horns and strings and wood instruments rose to his ears, and the town band began to play at the far end of the crowded terrace below to the accompaniment of a very soft, deep-throated drum. Vezin was very sensitive to music, knew about it intelligently, and had even ventured, unknown to his friends, upon the composition of quiet melodies with low-running chords which he played to himself with the soft pedal when no one was about. And this music, floating up through the trees, from an invisible and doubtless very picturesque band of the townspeople, wholly charmed him. He recognized nothing that they played, and it sounded as though they were simply improvising without a conductor. No definitely marked time ran through the pieces, which ended and began oddly after the fashion of wind through an aeolian harp. It was part of the place and scene, just as the dying sunlight and faintly breathing wind were part of the scene and hour, and the mellow notes of old-fashioned, plaintive horns, pierced here and there by the sharper strings, all half smothered by the continuous booming of the deep drum, touched his soul with a curiously potent spell that was almost too engrossing to be quite pleasant.

There was a certain queer sense of bewitchment in it all. The music seemed to him oddly unartificial. It made him think of trees swept by the wind, of night breezes singing among wires and chimney-stacks, or in the rigging of invisible ships; or—and the simile leaped up in his thoughts with a sudden sharpness of suggestion—a chorus of animals, of wild creatures, somewhere in desolate places of the world, crying and singing as animals will, to the moon. He could fancy he heard the wailing, half-human cries of cats upon the tiles at night, rising and falling with weird intervals of sound,

and this music, muffled by distance and the trees, made him
think of a queer company of these creatures on some roof far away
in the sky, uttering their solemn music to one another and the
moon in chorus.

It was, he felt at the time, a singular image to occur to him, yet
it expressed his sensation pictorially better than anything else. The
instruments played such impossibly odd intervals, and the cre-
scendos and diminuendos were so very suggestive of cat-land on
the tiles at night, rising swiftly, dropping without warning to deep
notes again, and all in such strange confusion of discords and
accords. But, at the same time a plaintive sweetness resulted on the
whole, and the discords of these half-broken instruments were so
singular that they did not distress his musical soul like fiddles out
of tune.

He listened a long time, wholly surrendering himself as his character was, and then strolled homewards in the dusk as the air grew
chilly.

"There was nothing to alarm?" put in Dr Silence briefly.

"Absolutely nothing," said Vezin; "but you know it was all so
fantastical and charming that my imagination was profoundly impressed. Perhaps, too," he continued, gently explanatory, "it was
this stirring of my imagination that caused other impressions; for as
I walked back the spell of the place began to steal over me in a
dozen ways, though all intelligible ways. But there were other things
I could not account for in the least, even then."

"Incidents, you mean?"

"Hardly incidents, I think. A lot of vivid sensations crowded themselves upon my mind and I could trace them to no causes. It was
just after sunset and the tumbled old buildings traced magical outlines against an opalescent sky of gold and red. The dusk was running down the twisted streets. All round the hill the plain pressed
in like a dim sea, its level rising with the darkness. The spell of this
kind of scene, you know, can be very moving, and it was so that
night. Yet I felt that what came to me had nothing directly to do
with the mystery and wonder of the scene."

"Not merely the subtle transformations of the spirit that come
with beauty," put in the doctor, noticing his hesitation.

"Exactly," Vezin went on, duly encouraged and no longer so fearful of our smiles at his expense. "The impressions came from somewhere else. For instance, down the busy main street where men and women were bustling home from work, shopping at stalls and barrows, idly gossiping in groups, and all the rest of it, I saw that I aroused no interest and that no one turned to stare at me as a foreigner and stranger. I was utterly ignored, and my presence among them excited no special interest or attention.

"And then, quite suddenly, it dawned upon me with conviction that all the time this indifference and inattention were merely feigned. Everybody, as a matter of fact, was watching me closely. Every movement I made was known and observed. Ignoring me was all a pretence—an elaborate pretence."

He paused a moment and looked at us to see if we were smiling, and then continued, reassured—

"It is useless to ask me how I noticed this, because I simply cannot explain it. But the discovery gave me something of a shock. Before I got back to the inn, however, another curious thing rose up strongly in my mind and forced my recognition of it as true. And this too, I may as well say at once, was equally inexplicable to me. I mean I can only give you the fact, as fact it was to me."

The little man left his chair and stood on the mat before the fire. His diffidence lessened from now onwards, as he lost himself again in the magic of the old adventure. His eyes shone a little already as he talked.

"Well," he went on, his soft voice rising somewhat with his excitement, "I was in a shop when it came to me first—though the idea must have been at work for a long time subconsciously to appear in so complete a form all at once. I was buying socks, I think," he laughed, "and struggling with my dreadful French, when it struck me that the woman in the shop did not care two pins whether I bought anything or not. She was indifferent whether she made a sale or did not make a sale. She was only pretending to sell.

"This sounds a very small and fanciful incident to build upon what follows. But really it was not small. I mean it was the spark that lit the line of powder and ran along to the big blaze in my mind.

"For the whole town, I suddenly realized, was something other than I so far saw it. The real activities and interests of the people were elsewhere and otherwise than appeared. Their true lives lay somewhere out of sight behind the scenes. Their busy-ness was but the outward semblance that masked their actual purposes. They bought and sold, and ate and drank, and walked about the streets, yet all the while the main stream of their existence lay somewhere beyond my ken, underground, in secret places. In the shops and at the stalls they did not care whether I purchased their articles or not; at the inn, they were indifferent to my staying or going; their life lay remote from my own, springing from hidden, mysterious sources, coursing out of sight, unknown. It was all a great, elaborate pretence, assumed possibly for my benefit, or possibly for purposes of their own. But the main current of their energies ran elsewhere. I almost felt as an unwelcome foreign substance might be expected to feel when it has found its way into the human system, and the whole body organizes itself to eject it or to absorb it. The town was doing this very thing to me.

"This bizarre notion presented itself forcibly to my mind as I walked home to the inn, and I began busily to wonder wherein the true life of this town could lie and what were the actual interests and activities of its hidden life.

"And now that my eyes were partly opened, I noticed other things, too, that puzzled me, first of which, I think, was the extraordinary silence of the whole place. Positively, the town was muffled. Although the streets were paved with cobbles the people moved about silently, softly, with padded feet, like cats. Nothing made noise. All was hushed, subdued, muted. The very voices were quiet, low-pitched, like purring. Nothing clamorous, vehement, or emphatic seemed able to live in the drowsy atmosphere of soft dreaming that soothed this little hill-town into its sleep. It was like the woman at the inn—an outward repose screening intense inner activity and purpose.

"Yet there was no sign of lethargy or sluggishness anywhere about it. The people were active and alert. Only a magical and uncanny softness lay over them all like a spell."

Vezin passed his hand across his eyes for a moment as though the memory had become very vivid. His voice had run off into a whisper so that we heard the last part with difficulty. He was telling a true thing obviously, yet something that he both liked and hated telling.

"I went back to the inn," he continued presently in a louder voice, "and dined. I felt a new strange world about me. My old world of reality receded. Here, whether I liked it or no, was something new and incomprehensible. I regretted having left the train so impulsively. An adventure was upon me, and I loathed adventures as foreign to my nature. Moreover, this was the beginning apparently of an adventure somewhere deep within me, in a region I could not check or measure, and a feeling of alarm mingled itself with my wonder—alarm for the stability of what I had for forty years recognized as my 'personality'.

"I went upstairs to bed, my mind teeming with thoughts that were unusual to me, and of rather a haunting description. By way of relief I kept thinking of that nice, prosaic noisy train and all those wholesome, blustering passengers. I almost wished I were with them again. But my dreams took me elsewhere. I dreamed of cats, and soft-moving creatures, and the silence of life in a dim muffled world beyond the senses."

I I

Vezin stayed on from day to day, indefinitely, much longer than he had intended. He felt in a kind of dazed, somnolent condition. He did nothing in particular, but the place fascinated him and he could not decide to leave. Decisions were always very difficult for him and he sometimes wondered how he had ever brought himself to the point of leaving the train. It seemed as though someone else must have arranged it for him, and once or twice his thoughts ran to the swarthy Frenchman who had sat opposite. If only he could have understood that long sentence ending so strangely with "*à cause du sommeil et à cause des chats*". He wondered what it all meant.

Meanwhile the hushed softness of the town held him prisoner and he sought in his muddling, gentle way to find out where the mystery lay, and what it was all about. But his limited French and his constitutional hatred of active investigation made it hard for him to buttonhole anybody and ask questions. He was content to observe, and watch, and remain negative.

The weather held on calm and hazy, and this just suited him. He wandered about the town till he knew every street and alley. The people suffered him to come and go without let or hindrance, though it became clearer to him every day that he himself was never free from observation. The town watched him as a cat watches a mouse. And he got no nearer to finding out what they were all so busy with or where the main stream of their activities lay. This remained hidden. The people were as soft and mysterious as cats.

But that he was continually under observation became more evident from day to day.

For instance, when he strolled to the end of the town and entered a little green public garden beneath the ramparts and seated himself upon one of the empty benches in the sun, he was quite alone— at first. Not another seat was occupied; the little park was empty, the paths deserted. Yet, within ten minutes of his coming, there must have been fully twenty persons scattered about him, some strolling aimlessly along the gravel walks, staring at the flowers, and others seated on wooden benches enjoying the sun like himself. None of them appeared to take any notice of him; yet he understood quite well they had all come there to watch. They kept him under close observation. In the street they had seemed busy enough, hurrying upon various errands; yet these were suddenly all forgotten and they had nothing to do but loll and laze in the sun, their duties unremembered. Five minutes after he left, the garden was again deserted, the seats vacant. But in the crowded street it was the same thing again; he was never alone. He was ever in their thoughts.

By degrees, too, he began to see how it was he was so cleverly watched, yet without the appearance of it. The people did nothing *directly*. They behaved *obliquely*. He laughed in his mind as the thought thus clothed itself in words, but the phrase exactly described it. They looked at him from angles which naturally should have led their sight in another direction altogether. Their movements were oblique, too, so far as these concerned himself. The straight, direct thing was not their way evidently. They did nothing obviously. If he entered a shop to buy, the woman walked instantly away and busied herself with something at the farther end of the counter, though answering at once when he spoke, showing that she knew he was there and that this was her only way of attending to him. It was the fashion of the cat she followed. Even in the dining-room of the inn the be-whiskered and courteous waiter, lithe and silent in all his movements, never seemed able to come straight to his table for an order or a dish. He came by zigzags, indirectly, vaguely, so that he appeared to be going to another table altogether, and only turned suddenly at the last moment, and was there beside him.

Vezin smiled curiously to himself as he described how he began to realize these things. Other tourists there were none in the hostel, but he recalled the figures of one or two old men, inhabitants, who took their *déjeuner* and dinner there, and remembered how fantastically they entered the room in similar fashion. First, they paused in the doorway, peering about the room, and then, after a temporary inspection, they came in, as it were, sideways, keeping close to the walls, so that he wondered which table they were making for, and at the last minute making almost a little quick run to their particular seats. And again he thought of the ways and methods of cats.

Other small incidents, too, impressed him as all part of this queer, soft town with its muffled, indirect life, for the way some of the people appeared and disappeared with extraordinary swiftness puzzled him exceedingly. It may have been all perfectly natural, he knew, yet he could not make it out how the alleys swallowed them up and shot them forth in a second of time when there were no visible doorways or openings near enough to explain the phenomenon. Once he followed two elderly women who, he felt, had been particularly examining him across the street—quite near the inn this was—and saw them turn the corner a few feet only in front of him. Yet when he sharply followed on their heels he saw nothing but an utterly deserted alley stretching in front of him with no sign of a living thing. And the only opening through which they could have escaped was a porch some fifty yards away, which not the swiftest human runner could have reached in time.

And in just such sudden fashion people appeared when he never expected them. Once when he heard a great noise of fighting going on behind a low wall, and hurried up to see what was going on, what should he see but a group of girls and women engaged in vociferous conversation which instantly hushed itself to the normal whispering note of the town when his head appeared over the wall. And even then none of them turned to look at him directly, but slunk off with the most unaccountable rapidity into doors and sheds across the yard. And their voices, he thought, had sounded so like, so strangely like, the angry snarling of fighting animals, almost of cats.

The whole spirit of the town, however, continued to evade him as something elusive, protean, screened from the outer world, and at the same time intensely, genuinely vital; and, since he now formed part of its life, this concealment puzzled and irritated him; more— it began rather to frighten him.

Out of the mists that slowly gathered about his ordinary surface thoughts there rose again the idea that the inhabitants were waiting for him to declare himself, to take an attitude, to do this, or to do that; and that when he had done so they in their turn would at length make some direct response, accepting or rejecting him. Yet the vital matter concerning which his decision was awaited came no nearer to him.

Once or twice he purposely followed little processions or groups of the citizens in order to find out, if possible, on what purpose they were bent, but they always discovered him in time and dwindled away, each individual going his or her own way. It was always the same: he never could learn what their main interest was. The cathedral was ever empty, the old church of St. Martin, at the other end of the town, deserted. They shopped because they had to, and not because they wished to. The booths stood neglected, the stalls unvisited, the little cafés desolate. Yet the streets were always full, the townsfolk ever on the bustle.

"Can it be," he thought to himself, yet with a deprecating laugh that he should have dared to think anything so odd, "can it be that these people are people of the twilight, that they live only at night their real life, and come out honestly only with the dusk? That during the day they make a sham though brave pretence, and after the sun is down their true life begins? Have they the souls of night-things, and is the whole blessed town in the hands of the cats?"

The fancy somehow electrified him with little shocks of shrinking and dismay. Yet, though he affected to laugh, he knew that he was beginning to feel more than uneasy, and that strange forces were tugging with a thousand invisible chords at the very centre of his being. Something utterly remote from his ordinary life, something that had not waked for years, began faintly to stir in his soul, sending feelers abroad into his brain and heart, shaping queer thoughts and penetrating even into certain of his minor actions. Something exceedingly vital to himself, to his soul, hung in the balance.

And, always when he returned to the inn about the hour of sunset, he saw the figures of the townsfolk stealing through the dusk from their shop doors, moving sentry-wise to and fro at the corners of the streets, yet always vanishing silently like shadows at his near approach. And as the inn invariably closed its doors at ten o'clock he had never yet found the opportunity he rather half-heartedly sought to see for himself what account the town could give of itself at night.

"——à cause du sommeil et à cause des chats"—the words now rang in his ears more and more often, though still as yet without any definite meaning.

Moreover, something made him sleep like the dead.

III

It was, I think, on the fifth day—though in this detail his story sometimes varied—that he made a definite discovery which increased his alarm and brought him up to a rather sharp climax. Before that he had already noticed that a change was going forward and certain subtle transformations being brought about in his character which modified several of his minor habits. And he had affected to ignore them. Here, however, was something he could no longer ignore; and it startled him.

At the best of times he was never very positive, always negative rather, compliant and acquiescent; yet, when necessity arose he was capable of reasonably vigorous action and could take a strongish decision. The discovery he now made that brought him up with such a sharp turn was that this power had positively dwindled to nothing. He found it impossible to make up his mind. For, on this fifth day, he realized that he had stayed long enough in the town, and that for reasons he could only vaguely define to himself it was wiser *and safer* that he should leave.

And he found that he could not leave!

This is difficult to describe in words, and it was more by gesture and the expression of his face that he conveyed to Dr Silence the stage of impotence he had reached. All this spying and watching, he said, had, as it were, spun a net about his feet so that he was trapped and powerless to escape; he felt like a fly that had blundered into the intricacies of a great web; he was caught, imprisoned, and could not get away. It was a distressing sensation. A numbness had crept over his will till it had become almost incapable of decision. The mere thought of vigorous action—action towards escape— began to terrify him. All the currents of his life had turned inwards upon himself, striving to bring to the surface something that lay buried almost beyond reach, determined to force his recognition of something he had long forgotten—forgotten years upon years, centuries almost ago. It seemed as though a window deep within his being would presently open and reveal an entirely new world, yet somehow a world that was not unfamiliar. Beyond that, again, he fancied a great curtain hung; and when that, too, rolled up he would see still further into this region and at last understand something of the secret life of these extraordinary people.

"Is this why they wait and watch?" he asked himself with rather a shaking heart, "for the time when I shall join them—or refuse to join them? Does the decision rest with me, after all, and not with them?"

And it was at this point that the sinister character of the adventure first really declared itself, and he became genuinely alarmed.

The stability of his rather fluid little personality was at stake, he felt, and something in his heart turned coward.

Why otherwise should he have suddenly taken to walking stealthily, silently, making as little sound as possible, for ever looking behind him? Why else should he have moved almost on tiptoe about the passages of the practically deserted inn, and when he was abroad have found himself deliberately taking advantage of what cover presented itself? And why, if he was not afraid, should the wisdom of staying indoors after sundown have suddenly occurred to him as eminently desirable? Why, indeed?

And, when John Silence gently pressed him for an explanation of these things, he admitted apologetically that he had none to give.

"It was simply that I feared something might happen to me unless I kept a sharp look-out. I felt afraid. It was instinctive," was all he could say. "I got the impression that the whole town was after me—wanted me for something; and that if it got me I should lose myself, or at least the Self I knew, in some unfamiliar state of consciousness. But I am not a psychologist, you know," he added meekly, "and I cannot define it better than that."

It was while lounging in the courtyard half an hour before the evening meal that Vezin made this discovery, and he at once went upstairs to his quiet room at the end of the winding passage to think it over alone. In the yard it was empty enough, true, but there was always the possibility that the big woman whom he dreaded would come out of some door, with her pretence of knitting to sit and watch him. This had happened several times, and he could not endure the sight of her. He still remembered his original fancy, bizarre though it was, that she would spring upon him the moment his back was turned and land with one single crushing leap upon his neck. Of course it was nonsense, but then it haunted him, and once an idea begins to do that it ceases to be nonsense. It has clothed itself in reality.

He went upstairs accordingly. It was dusk, and the oil lamps had not yet been lit in the passages. He stumbled over the uneven surface of the ancient flooring, passing the dim outlines of doors along the corridor—doors that he had never once seen opened—rooms that seemed never occupied. He moved, as his habit now was, stealthily and on tiptoe.

Half-way down the last passage to his own chamber there was a sharp turn, and it was just here, while groping round the walls with outstretched hands, that his fingers touched something that was not wall—something that moved. It was soft and warm in texture, indescribably fragrant, and about the height of his shoulder; and he immediately thought of a furry, sweet-smelling kitten. The next minute he knew it was something quite different.

Instead of investigating, however—his nerves must have been too overwrought for that, he said—he shrank back as closely as possible against the wall on the other side. The thing, whatever it was, slipped past him with a sound of rustling, and retreated with light footsteps down the passage behind him, was gone. A breath of warm scented air was wafted to his nostrils.

Vezin caught his breath for an instant and paused, stock-still, half-leaning against the wall—and then almost ran down the remaining distance and entered his room with a rush, locking the door hurriedly behind him. Yet it was not fear that made him run: it was excitement, pleasurable excitement. His nerves were tingling, and a delicious glow made itself felt all over his body. In a flash it came to him that this was just what he had felt twenty-five years ago as a boy when he was in love for the first time. Warm currents of life ran all over him and mounted to his brain in a whirl of soft delight. His mood was suddenly become tender, melting, loving.

The room was quite dark, and he collapsed upon the sofa by the window, wondering what had happened to him and what it all meant. But the only thing he understood clearly in that instant was that something in him had swiftly, magically changed: he no longer wished to leave, or to argue with himself about leaving. The encounter in the passage-way had changed all that. The strange perfume of it still hung about him, bemusing his heart and mind. For he knew that it was a girl who had passed him, a girl's face that his fingers had brushed in the darkness, and he felt in some extraordinary way as though he had been actually kissed by her, kissed full upon the lips.

Trembling, he sat upon the sofa by the window and struggled

to collect his thoughts. He was utterly unable to understand how the mere passing of a girl in the darkness of a narrow passage-way could communicate so electric a thrill to his whole being that he still shook with the sweetness of it. Yet, there it was! And he found it as useless to deny as to attempt analysis. Some ancient fire had entered his veins, and now ran coursing through his blood; and that he was forty-five instead of twenty did not matter one little jot. Out of all the inner turmoil and confusion emerged the one salient fact that the mere atmosphere, the merest casual touch, of this girl, unseen, unknown in the darkness, had been sufficient to stir dormant fires in the centre of his heart, and rouse his whole being from a state of feeble sluggishness to one of tearing and tumultuous excitement.

After a time, however, the number of Vezin's years began to assert their cumulative power; he grew calmer; and when a knock came at length upon his door and he heard the waiter's voice suggesting that dinner was nearly over, he pulled himself together and slowly made his way downstairs into the dining-room.

Everyone looked up as he entered, for he was very late, but he took his customary seat in the far corner and began to eat. The trepidation was still in his nerves, but the fact that he had passed through the court-yard and hall without catching sight of a petticoat served to calm him a little. He ate so fast that he had almost caught up with the current stage of the table d'hôte, when a slight commotion in the room drew his attention.

His chair was so placed that the door and the greater portion of the long *salle à manger* were behind him, yet it was not necessary to turn round to know that the same person he had passed in the dark passage had now come into the room. He felt the presence long before he heard or saw anyone. Then he became aware that the old men, the only other guests, were rising one by one in their places, and exchanging greetings with someone who passed among them from table to table. And when at length he turned with his heart beating furiously to ascertain for himself, he saw the form of a young girl, lithe and slim, moving down the centre of the room and making straight for his own table in the corner. She moved wonderfully, with sinuous grace, like a young panther, and her approach filled him with such delicious bewilderment that he was utterly unable to tell at first what her face was like, or discover what it was about the whole presentment of the creature that filled him anew with trepidation and delight.

"Ah, Ma'amselle est de retour!" he heard the old waiter murmur at his side, and he was just able to take in that she was the daughter of the proprietress, when she was upon him, and he heard her voice. She was addressing him. Something of red lips he saw and laughing white teeth, and stray wisps of fine dark hair about the temples; but all the rest was a dream in which his own emotions rose like a thick cloud before his eyes and prevented his seeing accurately, or knowing exactly what he did. He was aware that she greeted him with a charming little bow; that her beautiful large eyes looked searchingly into his own; that the perfume he had noticed in the dark passage again assailed his nostrils, and that she was bending a little towards him and leaning with one hand on the table at his side. She was quite close to him—that was the chief thing he knew—explaining that she had been asking after the comfort of her mother's guests, and was now introducing herself to the latest arrival—himself.

"M'sieur has already been here a few days," he heard the waiter say; and then her own voice sweet as singing, replied:

"Ah, but M'sieur is not going to leave us just yet, I hope. My mother is too old to look after the comfort of our guests properly, but now I am here I will remedy all that." She laughed deliciously. "M'sieur shall be well looked after."

Vezin, struggling with his emotion and desire to be polite, half rose to acknowledge the pretty speech, and to stammer some sort of reply, but as he did so his hand by chance touched her own that was resting upon the table, and a shock that was for all the world like a shock of electricity, passed from her skin into his body. His soul wavered and shook deep within him. He caught her eyes fixed upon his own with a look of most curious intentness, and the next moment he knew that he had sat down wordless again on his chair, that the girl was already half-way across the room, and that he was trying to eat his salad with a dessert-spoon and a knife.

Longing for her return, and yet dreading it, he gulped down the remainder of his dinner, and then went at once to his bedroom to be alone with his thoughts. This time the passages were lighted, and he suffered no exciting contretemps; yet the winding corridor was dim with shadows, and the last portion, from the bend of the walls onwards, seemed longer than he had ever known it. It ran downhill like the pathway on a mountain-side, and as he tiptoed softly down it he felt that by rights it ought to have led him clean out of the house into the heart of a great forest. The world was singing with him. Strange fancies filled his brain, and once in the room, with the door securely locked, he did not light the candles, but sat by the open window thinking long, long thoughts that came unbidden in troops to his mind.

This part of the story he told to Dr. Silence, without special coaxing, it is true, yet with much stammering embarrassment. He could not in the least understand, he said, how the girl had managed to affect him so profoundly, and even before he had set eyes upon her. For her mere proximity in the darkness had been sufficient to set him on fire. He knew nothing of enchantments, and for years had been a stranger to anything approaching tender relations with any member of the opposite sex, for he was encased in shyness, and realized his overwhelming defects only too well. Yet this bewitching young creature came to him deliberately. Her manner was unmistakable, and she sought him out on every possible occasion. Chaste and sweet she was undoubtedly, yet frankly inviting; and she won him utterly with the first glance of her shining eyes, even if she had not already done so in the dark merely by the magic of her invisible presence.

"You felt she was altogether wholesome and good?" queried the doctor. "You had no reaction of any sort—for instance, of alarm?"

Vezin looked up sharply with one of his inimitable little apologetic smiles. It was some time before he replied. The mere memory of the adventure had suffused his shy face with blushes, and his brown eyes sought the floor again before he answered.

"I don't think I can quite say that," he explained presently. "I acknowledged certain qualms, sitting up in my room afterwards. A conviction grew upon me that there was something about her—how shall I express it?—well, something unholy. It is not impurity in any

sense, physical or mental, that I mean, but something quite indefinable that gave me a vague sensation of the creeps. She drew me, and
at the same time repelled me, more than—than—"

He hesitated, blushing furiously, and unable to finish the sentence.

"Nothing like it has ever come to me before or since," he concluded with lame confusion. "I suppose it was, as you suggested just
now, something of an enchantment. At any rate, it was strong
enough to make me feel that I would stay in that awful little haunted
town for years if only I could see her every day, hear her voice,
watch her wonderful movements, and sometimes, perhaps, touch her
hand."

"Can you explain to me what you felt was the source of her
power?" John Silence asked, looking purposely anywhere but at the
narrator.

"I am surprised that *you* should ask me such a question,"
answered Vezin, with the nearest approach to dignity he could
manage. "I think no man can describe to another convincingly
wherein lies the magic of the woman who ensnares him. I certainly
cannot. I can only say this slip of a girl bewitched me, and the
mere knowledge that she was living and sleeping in the same house
filled me with an extraordinary sense of delight.

"But there's one thing I can tell you," he went on earnestly, his
eyes aglow, "namely, that she seemed to sum up and synthesize in
herself all the strange hidden forces that operated so mysteriously
in the town and its inhabitants. She had the silken movements of
the panther, going smoothly, silently, to and fro, and the same
indirect, oblique methods as the townsfolk, screening, like them,
secret purposes of her own—purposes that I was sure had *me* for
their objective. She kept me, to my terror and delight, ceaselessly
under observation, yet so carelessly, so consummately, that another
man less sensitive, if I may say so"—he made a deprecating gesture
"or less prepared by what had gone before, would never have
noticed it all. She was always still, always reposeful, yet she seemed
to be everywhere at once, so that I never could escape from her. I
was continually meeting the stare and laughter of her great eyes,
in the corners of the rooms, in the passages, calmly looking at me
through the windows, or in the busiest parts of the public streets."

Their intimacy, it seems, grew very rapidly after this first encounter which had so violently disturbed the little man's equilibrium.
He was naturally very prim, and prim folk live mostly in so small
a world that anything violently unusual may shake them clean out
of it, and they therefore instinctively distrust originality. But Vezin
began to fórget his primness after a while. The girl was always
modestly behaved, and as her mother's representative she naturally
had to be with the guests in the hotel. It was not out of the way that
a spirit of camaraderie should spring up. Besides, she was young,
she was charmingly pretty, she was French, and—she obviously
liked him.

At the same time, there was something indescribable—a certain
indefinable atmosphere of other places, other times—that made
him try hard to remain on his guard, and sometimes made him
catch his breath with a sudden start. It was all rather like a delirious
dream, half delight, half dread, he confided in a whisper to Dr
Silence; and more than once he hardly knew quite what he was
doing or saying, as though he were driven forward by impulses he
scarcely recognized as his own.

And though the thought of leaving presented itself again and
again to his mind, it was each time with less insistence, so that he
stayed on from day to day, becoming more and more a part of the
sleepy life of this dreamy medieval town, losing more and more of
his recognizable personality. Soon, he felt, the curtain within would
roll up with an awful rush, and he would find himself suddenly
admitted into the secret purposes of the hidden life that lay behind
it all. Only, by that time, he would have become transformed into
an entirely different being.

And, meanwhile, he noticed various little signs of the intention to
make his stay attractive to him: flowers in his bedroom, a more
comfortable arm-chair in the corner, and even special little extra
dishes on his private table in the dining-room. Conversations, too,
with "Mademoiselle Ilsé" became more and more frequent and
pleasant, and although they seldom travelled beyond the weather, or
the details of the town, the girl, he noticed, was never in a hurry to
bring them to an end, and often contrived to inject little odd

sentences that he never properly understood, yet felt to be significant.

And it was these stray remarks, full of a meaning that evaded him, that pointed to some hidden purpose of her own and made him feel uneasy. They all had to do, he felt sure, with reasons for his staying on in the town indefinitely.

"And has M'sieur not even yet come to a decision?" she said softly in his ear, sitting beside him in the sunny yard before *déjeuner*, the acquaintance having progressed with significant rapidity. "Because, if it's so difficult, we must all try together to help him!"

The question startled him, following upon his own thoughts. It was spoken with a pretty laugh, and a stray bit of hair across one eye, as she turned and peered at him half roguishly. Possibly he did not quite understand the French of it, for her near presence always confused his small knowledge of the language distressingly. Yet the words, and her manner, and something else that lay behind it all in her mind, frightened him. It gave such point to his feeling that the town was waiting for him to make up his mind on some important matter.

At the same time her voice, and the fact that she was there so close beside him in her soft dark dress, thrilled him inexpressibly.

"It is true I find it difficult to leave," he stammered, losing his way deliciously in the depth of her eyes, "and especially now that Mademoiselle Ilsé has come."

He was surprised at the success of his sentence, and quite delighted with the little gallantry of it. But at the same time he could have bitten his tongue off for having said it.

"Then, after all, you like our little town, or you would not be pleased to stay on," she said, ignoring the compliment.

"I am enchanted with it, and enchanted with you," he cried, feeling that his tongue was somehow slipping beyond the control of his brain. And he was on the verge of saying all manner of other things of the wildest description, when the girl sprang lightly up from her chair beside him, and made to go.

"It is *soupe à l'oignon* today!" she cried, laughing back at him through the sunlight, "and I must go and see about it. Otherwise, you know, M'sieur will not enjoy his dinner, and then, perhaps, he will leave us!"

He watched her cross the court-yard, moving with all the grace and lightness of the feline race, and her simple black dress clothed her, he thought, exactly like the fur of the same supple species. She turned once to laugh to him from the porch with the glass door, and then stopped a moment to speak to her mother, who sat knitting, as usual, in her corner seat just inside the hall-way.

But how was it, then, that the moment his eye fell upon this un-gainly woman, the pair of them appeared suddenly as other than they were? Whence came that transforming dignity and sense of power that enveloped them both as by magic? What was it about that massive woman that made her appear instantly regal, and set her on a throne in some dark and dreadful scenery, wielding a sceptre over the red glare of some tempestuous orgy? And why did this slender stripling of a girl, graceful as a willow, lithe as a young leopard, assume suddenly an air of sinister majesty, and move with flame and smoke about her head, and the darkness of night beneath her feet?

Vezin caught his breath and sat there transfixed. Then, almost simultaneously with its appearance, the queer notion vanished again, and the sunlight of day caught them both, and he heard her laugh-ing to her mother about the *soupe à l'oignon*, and saw her glancing back at him over her dear little shoulder with a smile that made him think of a dew-kissed rose bending lightly before summer airs.

And, indeed, the onion soup was particularly excellent that day, because he saw another cover laid at his small table, and with fluttering heart heard the waiter murmur by way of explanation that "Ma'mselle Ilsé would honour M'sieur today at *déjeuner*, as the custom sometimes is with her mother's guests."

So actually she sat by him all through that delicious meal, talking quietly to him in easy French, seeing that he was well looked after, mixing the salad dressing, and even helping him with her own hand. And, later in the afternoon, while he was smoking in the court-yard, longing for a sight of her as soon as her duties were done, she came again to his side, and when he rose to meet her, she stood facing him a moment, full of a perplexing sweet shyness before she spoke.

"My mother thinks you ought to know more of the beauties of our little town, and *I* think so, too! Would M'sieur like me to be his guide, perhaps? I can show him everything, for our family has lived here for many generations."

She had him by the hand, indeed, before he could find a single word to express his pleasure, and led him, all unresisting, out into the street, yet in such a way that it seemed perfectly natural she should do so, and without the faintest suggestion of boldness or immodesty. Her face glowed with the pleasure and interest of it, and with her short dress and tumbled hair she looked every bit the charming child of seventeen that she was, innocent and playful, proud of her native town, and alive beyond her years to the sense of its ancient beauty.

So they went over the town together, and she showed what she considered its chief interest, the tumble-down old house where her forebears had lived; the sombre, aristocratic-looking mansion where her mother's family dwelt for centuries, and the ancient market-place where several hundred years before the witches had been burnt by the score. She kept up a lively running stream of talk about it all, of which he understood not a fiftieth part as he trudged along by her side, cursing his forty-five years and feeling all the yearnings of his early manhood revive and jeer at him. And, as she talked, England and Surbiton seemed very far away indeed, almost in another age of the world's history. Her voice touched something immeasurably old in him, something that slept deep. It lulled the surface parts of his consciousness to sleep, allowing what was far more ancient to awaken. Like the town, with its elaborate pretence of modern active life, the upper layers of his being became dulled, soothed, muffled, and what lay underneath began to stir in its sleep. That big Curtain swayed a little to and fro. Presently it might lift altogether . . .

He began to understand a little better at last. The mood of the town was reproducing itself in him. In proportion as his ordinary external self became muffled, that inner secret life, that was far more real and vital, asserted itself. And this girl was surely the high priestess of it all, the chief instrument of its accomplishment. New thoughts, with new interpretations, flooded his mind as she walked beside him through the winding streets, while the picturesque old gabled town, softly coloured in the sunset, had never appeared to him so wholly wonderful and seductive.

And only one curious incident came to disturb and puzzle him, slight in itself, but utterly inexplicable, bringing white terror into the child's face and a scream to her laughing lips. He had merely pointed to a column of blue smoke that rose from the burning autumn leaves and made a picture against the red roofs, and had then run to the wall and called her to his side to watch the flames shooting here and there through the heap of rubbish. Yet, at the sight of it, as though taken by surprise, her face had altered dreadfully, and she had turned and run like the wind, calling out wild sentences to him as she ran, of which he had not understood a single word except that the fire apparently frightened her, and she wanted to get quickly away from it, and to get him away too.

Yet five minutes later she was as calm and happy again as though nothing had happened to alarm or waken troubled thoughts in her, and they had both forgotten the incident.

They were looking over the ruined ramparts together, listening to the weird music of the band as he had heard it the first day of his arrival. It moved him again profoundly as it had done before, and somehow he managed to find his tongue and his best French. The girl leaned across the stones close beside him. No one was about. Driven by some remorseless engine within he began to stammer something—he hardly knew what—of his strange admiration for her. Almost at the first word she sprang lightly off the wall and came up, smiling, in front of him, just touching his knees as he sat there. She was hatless, as usual, and the sun caught her hair and one side of her cheek and throat.

"Oh, I'm *so* glad!" she cried, clapping her little hands softly in his face, "so very glad, because that means that if you like me you must also like what I do, and what I belong to."

Already he regretted bitterly having lost control of himself. Something in the phrasing of her sentence chilled him. He knew the fear of embarking upon an unknown and dangerous sea.

"You will take part in our real life, I mean," she added softly, with an indescribable coaxing of manner, as though she noticed his shrinking. "You will come back to us."

Already this slip of a child seemed to dominate him; he felt her power coming over him more and more; something emanated from her that stole over his senses and made him aware that her personality, for all its simple grace, held forces that were stately, imposing, august. He saw her again moving through smoke and flame amid broken and tempestuous scenery alarmingly strong, her terrible mother by her side. Dimly this shone through her smile and appearance of charming innocence.

"You will, I know," she repeated, holding him with her eyes.

They were quite alone up there on the ramparts, and the sensation that she was overmastering him stirred a wild sensuousness in his blood. The mingled abandon and reserve in her attracted him furiously, and all of him that was man rose up and resisted the creeping influence, at the same time acclaiming it with the full delight of his forgotten youth. An irresistible desire came to him to question her, to summon what still remained to him of his own little personality in an effort to retain the right to his normal self.

The girl had grown quiet again, and was now leaning on the broad wall close beside him, gazing out across the darkening plain, her elbows on the coping, motionless as a figure carved in stone. He took his courage in both hands.

"Tell me, Ilsé," he said, unconsciously imitating her own purring softness of voice, yet aware that he was utterly in earnest, "what is the meaning of this town, and what is this real life you speak of? And why is it that the people watch me from morning to night? Tell me what it all means! And tell me," he added more quickly with passion in his voice, "what you really are—yourself!"

She turned her head and looked at him through half-closed eyelids, her growing inner excitement betraying itself by the faint colour that ran like a shadow across her face.

"It seems to me"—he faltered oddly under her gaze—"that I have some right to know—"

Suddenly she opened her eyes to the full. "You love me, then?" she asked softly.

"I swear," he cried impetuously, moved as by the force of a rising tide, "I never felt before—I have never known any other girl who—"

"Then you *have* the right to know," she calmly interrupted his confused confession, "for love shares all secrets."

She paused, and a thrill like fire ran swiftly through him. Her words lifted him off the earth, and he felt a radiant happiness, followed almost the same instant in horrible contrast by the thought of death. He became aware that she had turned her eyes upon his own and was speaking again.

"The real life I speak of," she whispered, "is the old, old life within, the life of long ago, the life to which you, too, once belonged, and to which you still belong."

A faint wave of memory troubled the deeps of his soul as her low voice sank into him. What she was saying he knew instinctively to be true, even though he could not as yet understand its full purport. His present life seemed slipping from him as he listened, merging his personality in one that was far older and greater. It was this loss of his present self that brought to him the thought of death.

"You came here," she went on, "with the purpose of seeking it, and the people felt your presence and are waiting to know what you decide, whether you will leave them without having found it, or whether—"

Her eyes remained fixed upon his own, but her face began to change, growing larger and darker with an expression of age.

"It is their thoughts constantly playing about your soul that make you feel they watch you. They do not watch you with their eyes. The purposes of their inner life are calling to you, seeking to claim you. You were all part of the same life long, long ago, and now they want you back again among them."

Vezin's timid heart sank with dread as he listened; but the girl's eyes held him with a net of joy so that he had no wish to escape. She fascinated him, as it were, clean out of his normal self.

"Alone, however, the people could never have caught and held you," she resumed. "The motive force was not strong enough; it has faded through all these years. But I"—she paused a moment and looked at him with complete confidence in her splendid eyes— "I possess the spell to conquer you and hold you: the spell of old

love. I can win you back again and make you live the old life with
me, for the force of the ancient tie between us, if I choose to use it,
is irresistible. And I do choose to use it. I still want you. And you,
dear soul of my dim past"—she pressed closer to him so that her
breath passed across his eyes, and her voice positively sang—"I
mean to have you, for you love me and are utterly at my mercy."

Vezin heard, and yet did not hear; understood, yet did not
understand. He had passed into a condition of exaltation. The
world was beneath his feet, made of music and flowers, and he was
flying somewhere far above it through the sunshine of pure delight.
He was breathless and giddy with the wonder of her words. They
intoxicated him. And, still, the terror of it all, the dreadful thought
of death, pressed ever behind her sentences. For flames shot
through her voice out of black smoke and licked at his soul.

And they communicated with one another, it seemed to him by a
process of swift telepathy, for his French could never have com-
passed all he said to her. Yet she understood perfectly, and what
she said to him was like the recital of verses long since known. And
the mingled pain and sweetness of it as he listened were almost
more than his little soul could hold.

"Yet I came here wholly by chance—" he heard himself saying.

"No," she cried with passion, "you came here because I called to
you. I have called to you for years, and you came with the whole
force of the past behind you. You had to come, for I own you, and
I claim you."

She rose again and moved closer, looking at him with a certain
insolence in her face—the insolence of power.

The sun had set behind the towers of the old cathedral and the
darkness rose up from the plain and enveloped them. The music of
the band had ceased. The leaves of the plane-trees hung motionless,
but the chill of the autumn evening rose about them and made
Vezin shiver. There was no sound but the sound of their voices and
the occasional soft rustle of the girl's dress. He could hear the blood
rushing in his ears. He scarcely realized where he was or what he
was doing. Some terrible magic of the imagination drew him deeply
down into the tombs of his own being, telling him in no unfaltering
voice that her words shadowed forth the truth. And this simple little

French maid, speaking beside him with so strange authority, he saw curiously alter into quite another being. As he stared into her eyes, the picture in his mind grew and lived, dressing itself vividly to his inner vision with a degree of reality he was compelled to acknowledge. As once before, he saw her tall and stately, moving through wild and broken scenery of forests and mountain caverns, the glare of flames behind her head and clouds of shifting smoke about her feet. Dark leaves encircled her hair, flying loosely in the wind, and her limbs shone through the merest rags of clothing. Others were about her, too, and ardent eyes on all sides cast delirious glances upon her, but her own eyes were always for One only, one whom she held by the hand. For she was leading the dance in some tempestuous orgy to the music of chanting voices, and the dance she led circled about a great and awful Figure on a throne, brooding over the scene through lurid vapours, while innumerable other wild faces and forms crowded furiously about her in the dance. But the one she held by the hand he knew to be himself, and the monstrous shape upon the throne he knew to be her mother.

The vision rose within him, rushing to him down the long years of buried time, crying aloud to him with the voice of memory reawakened. And then the scene faded away, and he saw the clear circle of the girl's eyes gazing steadfastly into his own, and she became once more the pretty little daughter of the innkeeper, and he found his voice again.

"And you," he whispered tremblingly—"you child of visions and enchantment, how is it that you so bewitch me that I loved you even before I saw?"

She drew herself up beside him with an air of rare dignity.

"The call of the Past," she said; "and, besides," she added proudly, "in real life I am a princess—"

"A princess!" he cried.

"—and my mother is a queen!"

At this, little Vezin utterly lost his head. Delight tore at his heart and swept him into sheer ecstacy. To hear that sweet singing voice, and to see those adorable little lips utter such things, upset his balance beyond all hope of control. He took her in his arms and covered her unresisting face with kisses.

But even while he did so, and while the hot passion swept him, he felt that she was soft and loathsome, and that her answering kisses stained his very soul. . . . And when, presently, she had freed herself and vanished into the darkness, he stood there, leaning against the wall in a state of collapse, creeping with horror from the touch of her yielding body, and inwardly raging at the weakness that he already dimly realized must prove his undoing.

And from the shadows of the old buildings into which she disappeared there rose in the stillness of the night a singular, long-drawn cry, which at first he took for laughter, but which later he was sure he recognized as the almost human wailing of a cat.

IV

For a long time Vezin leant there against the wall, alone with his surging thoughts and emotions. He understood at length that he had done the one thing necessary to call down upon him the whole force of this ancient Past. For in those passionate kisses he had acknowledged the tie of olden days, and had revived it. And the memory of that soft impalpable caress in the darkness of the inn corridor came back to him with a shudder. The girl had first mastered him, and then led him to the one act that was necessary for her purpose. He had been waylaid, after the lapse of centuries—caught, and conquered.

Dimly he realized this, and sought to make plans for his escape. But, for the moment at any rate, he was powerless to manage his thoughts or will, for the sweet, fantastic madness of the whole adventure mounted to his brain like a spell, and he gloried in the feeling that he was utterly enchanted and moving in a world so much larger and wilder than the one he had ever been accustomed to.

The moon, pale and enormous, was just rising over the sea-like plain, when at last he rose to go. Her slanting rays drew all the houses into new perspective, so that their roofs, already glistening with dew, seemed to stretch much higher into the sky than usual, and their gables and quaint old towers lay far away in its purple reaches.

The cathedral appeared unreal in a silver mist. He moved softly, keeping to the shadows; but the streets were all deserted and very silent; the doors were closed, the shutters fastened. Not a soul was astir. The hush of night lay over everything; it was like a town of the dead, a churchyard with gigantic and grotesque tombstones.

Wondering where all the busy life of the day had so utterly disappeared, he made his way to a back door that entered the inn by means of the stables, thinking thus to reach his room unobserved. He reached the court-yard safely and crossed it by keeping close to the shadow of the wall. He sidled down it, mincing along on tiptoe, just as the old men did when they entered the *salle à manger*. He was horrified to find himself doing this instinctively. A strange impulse came to him, catching him somehow in the centre of his body—an impulse to drop upon all fours and run swiftly and silently. He glanced upwards and the idea came to him to leap up upon his window-sill overhead instead of going round by the stairs. This occurred to him as the easiest and most natural way. It was like the beginning of some horrible transformation of himself into something else. He was fearfully strung up.

The moon was higher now, and the shadows very dark along the side of the street where he moved. He kept among the deepest of them, and reached the porch with the glass doors.

But here there was light; the inmates, unfortunately, were still about. Hoping to slip across the hall unobserved and reach the stairs, he opened the door carefully and stole in. Then he saw that the hall was not empty. A large dark thing lay against the wall on his left. At first he thought it must be household articles. Then it moved, and he thought it was an immense cat, distorted in some way by the play of light and shadow. Then it rose straight up before him and he saw that it was the proprietress.

What she had been doing in this position he could only venture a dreadful guess, but the moment she stood up and faced him he was aware of some terrible dignity clothing her about that instantly recalled the girl's strange saying that she was a queen. Huge and sinister she stood there under the little oil lamp; alone with him in the empty hall. Awe stirred in his heart, and the roots of some ancient fear. He felt that he must bow to her and make some kind of obeisance. The impulse was fierce and irresistible, as of long habit. He glanced quickly about him. There was no one there. Then he deliberately inclined his head towards her. He bowed.

"*Enfin! M'sieur s'est donc décidé. C'est bien alors. J'en suis contente.*"

Her words came to him sonorously as through a great open space.

Then the great figure came suddenly across the flagged hall at him and seized his trembling hands. Some overpowering force moved with her and caught him.

"*On pourrait faire un p'tit tour ensemble, n'est-ce pas? Nous y allons cette nuit et il faut s'exercer un peu d'avance pour cela. Ilsé, Ilsé, viens donc ici. Viens vite!*"

And she whirled him round in the opening steps of some dance that seemed oddly and horribly familiar. They made no sound on the stones, this strange assorted couple. It was all soft and stealthy. And presently, when the air seemed to thicken like smoke, and a red glare as of flame shot through it, he was aware that somone else had joined them and that his hand the mother had released was now tightly held by the daughter. Ilsé had come in answer to the call, and he saw her with leaves of vervain twined in her dark hair, clothed in tattered vestiges of some curious garment, beautiful as the night, and horribly, odiously, loathsomely seductive.

"To the Sabbath! To the Sabbath!" they cried. "On to the Witches' Sabbath!"

Up and down that narrow hall they danced, the women on each side of him, to the wildest measure he had ever imagined, yet which he dimly, dreadfully remembered, till the lamp on the wall flickered and went out, and they were left in total darkness. And the devil woke in his heart with a thousand vile suggestions and made him afraid.

Suddenly they released his hand and he heard the voice of the mother cry that it was time, and they must go. Which way they went he did not pause to see. He only realized that he was free, and he blundered through the darkness till he found the stairs and then tore up them to his room as though all hell was at his heels.

He flung himself on the sofa, with his face in his hands, and groaned. Swiftly reviewing a dozen ways of immediate escape, all equally impossible, he finally decided that the only thing to do for the moment was to sit quiet and wait. He must see what was going to happen. At least in the privacy of his own bedroom he would be fairly safe. The door was locked. He crossed over and softly opened the window which gave upon the court-yard and also permitted a partial view of the hall through the glass doors.

As he did so the hum and murmur of a great activity reached his ears from the streets beyond—the sound of footsteps and voices muffled by distance. He leaned out cautiously and listened. The moonlight was clear and strong now, but his own window was in shadow, the silver disc being still behind the house. It came to him irresistibly that the inhabitants of the town, who a little while before had all been invisible behind closed doors, were now issuing forth, busy upon some secret and unholy errand. He listened intently.

At first everything about him was silent, but soon he became aware of movements going on in the house itself. Rustlings and creepings came to him across that still, moonlit yard. A concourse of living beings sent the hum of their activity into the night. Things were on the move everywhere. A biting pungent odour rose through the air, coming he knew not whence. Presently his eyes became glued to the windows of the opposite wall where the moonshine fell in a soft blaze. The roof overhead, and behind him, was reflected clearly in the panes of glass, and he saw the outlines of dark bodies moving with long footsteps over the tiles and along the coping. They passed swiftly and silently, shaped like immense cats, in an endless procession across the pictured glass, and then appeared to leap down to a lower level where he lost sight of them. He just caught the soft thudding of their leaps. Sometimes their shadows fell upon the white wall opposite, and then he could not make out whether they were the shadows of human beings or of cats. They seemed to change swiftly from one to the other. The transformation looked horribly real, for they leaped like human beings, yet changed swiftly in the air immediately afterwards, and dropped like animals.

The yard, too, beneath him, was now alive with the creeping movements of dark forms all stealthily drawing towards the porch with the glass doors. They kept so closely to the wall that he could not determine their actual shape, but when he saw that they passed on to the great congregation that was gathering in the hall, he understood that these were the creatures whose leaping shadows he had first seen reflected in the window-panes opposite. They were coming from all parts of the town, reaching the appointed meeting-place across the roofs and tiles, and springing from level to level till they came to the yard.

Then a new sound caught his ear, and he saw that the windows all about him were being softly opened, and that to each window came a face. A moment later figures began dropping hurriedly down into the yard. And these figures, as they lowered themselves down from the windows, were human, he saw; but once safely in the yard they fell upon all fours and changed in the swiftest possible second into—cats—huge, silent cats. They ran in streams to join the main body in the hall beyond.

So, after all, the rooms in the house had not been empty and unoccupied.

Moreover, what he saw no longer filled him with amazement. For he remembered it all. It was familiar. It had all happened before just so, hundreds of times, and he himself had taken part in it and known the wild madness of it all. The outline of the old building changed, the yard grew larger, and he seemed to be staring down upon it from a much greater height through smoky vapours. And, as he looked, half remembering, the old pains of long ago, fierce and sweet, furiously assailed him, and the blood stirred horribly as he heard the Call of the Dance again in his heart and tasted the ancient magic of Ilsé whirling by his side.

Suddenly he started back. A great lithe cat had leaped softly up from the shadows below on to the sill close to his face, and was staring fixedly at him with the eyes of a human. "Come," it seemed to say, "come with us to the Dance! Change as of old! Transform yourself swiftly and come!" Only too well he understood the creature's soundless call.

It was gone again in a flash with scarcely a sound of its padded feet on the stones, and then others dropped by the score down the side of the house, past his very eyes, all changing as they fell, and darting away rapidly, softly, towards the gathering point. And again he felt the dreadful desire to do likewise; to murmur the old incantation, and then drop upon hands and knees and run swiftly for the great flying leap into the air. Oh, how the passion of it rose within him like a flood, twisting his very entrails, sending his heart's desire flaming forth into the night for the old, old Dance of the Sorcerers at the Witches' Sabbath! The whirl of the stars was about him; once more he met the magic of the moon. The power of the wind, rushing from precipice and forest, leaping from cliff to cliff across the valleys, tore him away. . . . He heard the cries of the dancers and their wild laughter, and with this savage girl in his embrace he danced furiously about the dim throne where sat the Figure with the sceptre of majesty. . . .

Then, suddenly, all became hushed and still, and the fever died a little in his heart. The calm moonlight flooded a court-yard empty and deserted. They had started. The procession was off into the sky. And he was left behind—alone.

Vezin tiptoed softly across the room and unlocked the door. The murmur from the streets, growing momentarily as he advanced, met his ears. He made his way with the utmost caution down the corridor. At the head of the stairs he paused and listened. Below him, the hall where they had gathered was dark and still, but through opened doors and windows on the far side of the building came the sound of a great throng moving farther and farther into the distance.

He made his way down the creaking wooden stairs, dreading yet longing to meet some straggler who should point the way, but finding no one; across the dark hall, so lately thronged with living, moving things, and out through the opened front doors into the street. He could not believe that he was really left behind, really forgotten, that he had been purposely permitted to escape. It perplexed him.

Nervously he peered about him, and up and down the street; then, seeing nothing, advanced slowly down the pavement.

The whole town, as he went, showed itself empty and deserted, as though a great wind had blown everything alive out of it. The doors and windows of the houses stood open to the night; nothing stirred; moonlight and silence lay over all. The night lay about him like a cloak. The air, soft and cool, caressed his cheek like the touch of a great furry paw. He gained confidence and began to walk quickly, though still keeping to the shadowed side. Nowhere could he discover the faintest sign of the great unholy exodus he knew had just taken place. The moon sailed high over all in a sky cloudless and serene.

Hardly realizing where he was going, he crossed the open market-place and so came to the ramparts, whence he knew a pathway descended to the high road and along which he could make good his escape to one of the other little towns that lay to the northward, and so to the railway.

But first he paused and gazed out over the scene at his feet where the great plain lay like a silver map of some dream country. The still beauty of it entered his heart, increasing his sense of bewilder-ment and unreality. No air stirred, the leaves of the plane-trees stood motionless, the near details were defined with the sharpness of day against dark shadows, and in the distance the fields and woods melted away into haze and shimmering mistiness.

But the breath caught in his throat and he stood stock-still as though transfixed when his gaze passed from the horizon and fell upon the near prospect in the depth of the valley at his feet. The whole lower slopes of the hill, that lay hid from the brightness of the moon, were aglow, and through the glare he saw countless moving forms, shifting thick and fast between the openings of the trees; while overhead, like leaves driven by the wind, he discerned flying shapes that hovered darkly one moment against the sky and then settled down with cries and weird singing through the branches into the region that was aflame.

Spellbound, he stood and stared for a time that he could not measure. And then, moved by one of the terrible impulses that seemed to control the whole adventure, he climbed swiftly upon the top of the broad coping, and balanced a moment where the valley gaped at his feet. But in that very instant, as he stood hovering, a sudden movement among the shadows of the houses caught his eye, and he turned to see the outline of a large animal dart swiftly across the open space behind him, and land with a flying leap upon the top of the wall a little lower down. It ran like the wind to his feet and then rose up beside him upon the ramparts. A shiver seemed to run through the moonlight, and his sight trembled for a second.

His heart pulsed fearfully. Ilsé stood beside him, peering into his face.

Some dark substance, he saw, stained the girl's face and skin, shining in the moonlight as she stretched her hands towards him; she was dressed in wretched tattered garments that yet became her mightily; rue and vervain twined about her temples; her eyes glistened with unholy light. He only just controlled the wild impulse to take her in his arms and leap with her from their giddy perch into the valley below.

"See!" she cried, pointing with an arm on which the rags fluttered in the rising wind towards the forest aglow in the distance. "See where they await us! The woods are alive! Already the Great Ones are there, and the dance will soon begin! The salve is here! Anoint yourself and come!"

Though a moment before the sky was clear and cloudless, yet even while she spoke the face of the moon grew dark and the wind began to toss in the crests of the plane-trees at his feet. Stray gusts brought the sounds of hoarse singing and crying from the lower slopes of the hill, and the pungent odour he had already noticed about the court-yard of the inn rose about him in the air.

"Transform, transform!" she cried again, her voice rising like a song. "Rub well your skin before you fly. Come! Come with me to the Sabbath, to the madness of its furious delight, to the sweet and the terrible Sacraments prepared. The Throne is occupied. Anoint and come! Anoint and come!"

She grew to the height of a tree beside him, leaping upon the wall with flaming eyes and hair strewn upon the night. He, too, began to change swiftly. Her hands touched the skin of his face and neck, streaking him with the burning salve that sent the old magic into his blood with the power before which fades all that is good.

A wild roar came up to his ears from the heart of the wood, and the girl, when she heard it, leaped upon the wall in a frenzy of her wicked joy.

"Satan is there!" she screamed, rushing upon him and striving to draw him with her to the edge of the wall. "Satan has come! The Sacraments call us! Come, with your dear apostate soul, and we will worship and dance till the moon dies and the world is forgotten!"

Just saving himself from the dreadful plunge, Vezin struggled to release himself from her grasp, while the passion tore at his veins and all but mastered him. He shrieked aloud, not knowing what he said, and then he shrieked again. It was the old impulses, the old awful habits instinctively finding voice; for though it seemed to him that he merely shrieked nonsense, the words he uttered really had meaning in them, and were intelligible. It was the ancient call. And it was heard below. It was answered.

The wind whistled at the skirts of his coat as the air round him darkened with many flying forms crowding upwards out of the valley. The crying of hoarse voices smote upon his ears, coming closer. Strokes of wind buffeted him, tearing him this way and that along the crumbling top of the stone wall; and Ilsé clung to him with her long shining arms, smooth and bare holding him fast about the neck. But not Ilsé alone, for a dozen of them surrounded him, dropping out of the air. The pungent odour of the anointed bodies stifled him, exciting him to the old madness of the Sabbath, the dance of the witches and sorcerers doing honour to the personified Evil of the world.

"Anoint and away! Anoint and away!" they cried in wild chorus about him. "To the Dance that never dies! To the sweet and fearful fantasy of evil!"

Another moment and he would have yielded and gone, for his will turned soft and the flood of passionate memory all but overwhelmed him, when—so can a small thing alter the whole course of an adventure—he caught his foot upon a loose stone in the edge of the wall, and then fell with a sudden crash on to the ground below. But he fell towards the houses, in the open space of dust and cobble stones, and fortunately not into the gaping depth of the valley on the farther side.

And they, too, came in a tumbling heap about him, like flies upon a piece of food, but as they fell he was released for a moment from the power of their touch, and in that brief instant of freedom there flashed into his mind the sudden intuition that saved him. Before he could regain his feet he saw them scrabbling awkwardly back upon the wall, as though bat-like they could only fly by dropping from a height, and had no hold upon him in the open. Then, seeing them perched there in a row like cats upon a roof, all dark and singularly shapeless, their eyes like lamps, the sudden memory came back to him of Ilsé's terror at the sight of fire.

Quick as a flash he found his matches and lit the dead leaves that lay under the wall.

Dry and withered, they caught fire at once, and the wind carried the flame in a long line down the length of the wall, licking upwards as it ran; and with shrieks and wailings, the crowded row of forms upon the top melted away into the air on the other side, and were gone with a great rush and whirring of their bodies down into the heart of the haunted valley, leaving Vezin breathless and shaken in the middle of the deserted ground.

"Ilsé!" he called feebly; "Ilsé!" for his heart ached to think that she was really gone to the great Dance without him, and that he had lost the opportunity of its fearful joy. Yet at the same time his relief was so great, and he was so dazed and troubled in mind with the whole thing, that he hardly knew what he was saying, and only cried aloud in the fierce storm of his emotion . . .

The fire under the wall ran its course, and the moonlight came out again, soft and clear, from its temporary eclipse. With one last shuddering look at the ruined ramparts, and a feeling of horrid wonder for the haunted valley beyond, where the shapes still crowded and flew, he turned his face towards the town and slowly made his way in the direction of the hotel.

And as he went, a great wailing of cries, and a sound of howling, followed him from the gleaming forest below, growing fainter and fainter with the bursts of wind as he disappeared between the houses.

V

"It may seem rather abrupt to you, this sudden tame ending," said Arthur Vezin, glancing with flushed face and timid eyes at Dr Silence sitting there with his notebook, "but the fact is—er—from that moment my memory seems to have failed rather. I have no distinct recollection of how I got home or what precisely I did.

"It appears I never went back to the inn at all. I only dimly recollect racing down a long white road in the moonlight, past woods and villages, still and deserted, and then the dawn came up, and I saw the towers of a biggish town and so came to the station.

"But, long before that, I remember pausing somewhere on the road and looking back to where the hill-town of my adventure stood up in the moonlight, and thinking how exactly like a great monstrous cat it lay there upon the plain, its huge front paws lying down the two main streets, and the twin and broken towers of the cathedral marking its torn ears against the sky. That picture stays in my mind with the utmost vividness to this day.

"Another thing remains in my mind from that escape—namely, the sudden sharp reminder that I had not paid my bill, and the decision I made, standing there on the dusty highroad, that the baggage I had left behind would more than settle for my indebtedness.

"For the rest, I can only tell you that I got coffee and bread at a café on the outskirts of this town I had come to, and soon after found my way to the station and caught a train later in the day. That same evening I reached London."

"And how long altogether," asked John Silence quietly, "do you think you stayed in the town of the adventure?"

Vezin looked up sheepishly.

"I was coming to that," he resumed, with apologetic wrigglings of his body. "In London I found that I was a whole week out in reckoning of time. I had stayed over a week in the town, and it ought to have been September 15th—instead of which it was only September 10th!"

"So that, in reality, you had only stayed a night or two in the inn?" queried the doctor.

Vezin hesitated before replying. He shuffled upon the mat.

"I must have gained time somewhere," he said at length—"somewhere or somehow. I certainly had a week to my credit. I can't explain it. I can only give you the fact."

"And this happened to you last year, since when you have never been back to the place?"

"Last autumn, yes," murmured Vezin; "and I have never dared to go back. I think I never want to."

"And, tell me," asked Dr Silence at length, when he saw that the little man had evidently come to the end of his words and had nothing more to say, "had you ever read up the subject of the old witchcraft practices during the Middle Ages, or been at all interested in the subject?"

"Never!" declared Vizen emphatically. "I had never given a thought to such matters so far as I know—"

"Or to the question of reincarnation, perhaps?"

"Never—before my adventure; but I have since," he replied significantly.

There was, however, something still on the man's mind that he wished to relieve himself of by confession, yet could with difficulty bring himself to mention; and it was only after the sympathetic tactfulness of the doctor had provided numerous openings that he at length availed himself of one of them, and stammered that he would like to show him the marks he still had on his neck where, he said, the girl had touched him with her anointed hands.

He took off his collar after infinite fumbling hesitation, and lowered his shirt a little for the doctor to see. And there, on the surface of the skin, lay a faint reddish line across the shoulder and extending a little way down the back towards the spine. It certainly indicated exactly the position an arm might have taken in the act of embracing. And on the other side of the neck, slightly higher up, was a similar mark, though not quite so clearly defined.

"That was where she held me that night on the ramparts," he whispered, a strange light coming and going in his eyes.

It was some weeks later when I again found occasion to consult John Silence concerning another extraordinary case that had come under my notice, and we fell to discussing Vezin's story. Since hearing it, the doctor had made investigations on his own account, and one of his secretaries had discovered that Vezin's ancestors had actually lived for generations in the very town where the adventure came to him. Two of them, both women, had been tried and convicted as witches, and had been burned alive at the stake. Moreover, it had not been difficult to prove that the very inn where Vezin stayed was built about 1700 upon the spot where the funeral pyres stood and the executions took place. The town was a sort of head-quarters for all the sorcerers and witches of the entire region, and after conviction they were burnt there literally by scores.

"It seems strange," continued the doctor, "that Vezin should have remained ignorant of all this; but, on the other hand, it was not the kind of history that successive generations would have been anxious to keep alive, or to repeat to their children. Therefore I am inclined to think he still knows nothing about it.

"The whole adventure seems to have been a very vivid revival of the memories of an earlier life, caused by coming directly into con-tact with the living forces still intense enough to hang about the place, and, by a most singular chance too, with the very souls who had taken part with him in the events of that particular life. For the mother and daughter who impressed him so strangely must have been leading actors, with himself, in the scenes and practices of witchcraft which at that period dominated the imaginations of the whole country.

"One has only to read the histories of the times to know that these witches claimed the power of transforming themselves into various animals, both for the purpose of disguise and also to con-vey themselves swiftly to the scenes of their imaginary orgies. Lycanthropy, or the power to change themselves into wolves, was everywhere believed in, and the ability to transform themselves into cats by rubbing their bodies with a special salve or ointment pro-vided by Satan himself, found equal credence. The witchcraft trials abound in evidences of such universal beliefs."

Dr Silence quoted chapter and verse from many writers on the subject, and showed how every detail of Vezin's adventure had a basis in the practices of those dark days.

"But that the entire affair took place subjectively in the man's own consciousness, I have no doubt," he went on, in reply to my questions; "for my secretary who has been to the town to investigate, discovered his signature in the visitors' book, and proved by it that he had arrived on September 8th, and left suddenly without paying his bill. He left two days later, and they still were in possession of his dirty brown bag and some tourist clothes. I paid a few francs in settlement of his debt, and have sent his luggage on to him. The daughter was absent from home, but the proprietress, a large woman very much as he described her, told my secretary that he had seemed a very strange, absent-minded kind of gentleman, and after his disappearance she had feared for a long time that he had met with a violent end in the neighbouring forest where he used to roam about alone.

"I should like to have obtained a personal interview with the daughter so as to ascertain how much was subjective and how much actually took place with her as Vezin told it. For her dread of fire and the sight of burning must, of course, have been the intuitive memory of her former painful death at the stake, and have thus explained why he fancied more than once that he saw her through smoke and flame."

"And that mark on his skin, for instance?" I inquired.

"Merely the marks produced by hysterical brooding," he replied, "like the stigmata of the *religieuses,* and the bruises which appear on the bodies of hypnotized subjects who have been told to expect them. This is very common and easily explained. Only it seems curious that these marks should have remained so long in Vezin's case. Usually they disappear quickly."

"Obviously he is still thinking about it all, brooding, and living it all over again," I ventured.

"Probably. And this makes me fear that the end of his trouble is not yet. We shall hear of him again. It is a case, alas! I can do little to alleviate."

Dr Silence spoke gravely and with sadness in his voice.

"And what do you make of the Frenchman in the train?" I asked further—"the man who warned him against the place, *à cause du sommeil et à cause des chats*? Surely a very singular incident?"

"A *very* singular incident indeed," he made answer slowly, "and one I can only explain on the basis of a highly improbable coincidence—"

"Namely?"

"That the man was one who had himself stayed in the town and undergone there a similar experience. I should like to find this man and ask him. But the crystal is useless here, for I have no slightest clue to go upon, and I can only conclude that some singular psychic affinity, some force still active in his being out of the same past life, drew him thus to the personality of Vezin, and enabled him to fear what might happen to him, and thus to warn him as he did.

"Yes," he presently continued, half talking to himself, "I suspect in this case that Vezin was swept into the vortex of forces arising out of the intense activities of a past life, and that he lived over again a scene in which he had often played a leading part centuries before. For strong actions set up forces that are so slow to exhaust themselves, they may be said in a sense never to die. In this case they were not vital enough to render the illusion complete, so that the little man found himself caught in a very distressing confusion of the present and the past; yet he was sufficiently sensitive to recognize that it was true, and to fight against the degradation of returning, even in memory, to a former and lower state of development.

"Ah yes!" he continued, crossing the floor to gaze at the darkening sky, and seemingly quite oblivious of my presence, "subliminal uprushes of memory like this can be exceedingly painful, and sometimes exceedingly dangerous. I only trust that this gentle soul may soon escape from this obsession of a passionate and tempestuous past. But I doubt it, I doubt it."

His voice was hushed with sadness as he spoke, and when he turned back into the room again there was an expression of profound yearning upon his face, the yearning of a soul whose desire to help is sometimes greater than his power.

TOBERMORY

by Saki

T H E S C O T T I S H W R I T E R *Hector Hugh Munro (1870–*
1916), better known as Saki, *was a great lover of Cats. He had*
many of his own and, whilst in Burma, kept as a pet a tiger cub.
In an essay on the Cat he wrote, "the innate savage spirit that
helped its survival in the bygone days of tooth and claw may be
summoned forth from beneath the sleek exterior and the
torture-instinct (common alone to human and feline) may find
free play in the death-throes of some luckless bird or rodent".
It is interesting to apply this observation to Saki's own work
—particularly those stories which satirically use the Edwardian
social scene as a background. Such stories are elegant and
playful yet inevitably climax with a mordant denouement:
the velvet fur hides sharp claws.

Saki's stories read just as well today as when they were
written and in his cruel wit and bizarre situations he some-
times anticipated such later developments as Black Humour
and the Theatre of the Absurd.

Like William Hope Hodgson and many other gifted writers,
Saki died in action during the First World War.

It was a chill, rain-washed afternoon of a late August day, that
indefinite season when partridges are still in security or cold
storage, and there is nothing to hunt—unless one is bounded on the
north by the Bristol Channel, in which case one may lawfully gallop
after fat red stags. Lady Blemley's house-party was not bounded on
the north by the Bristol Channel, hence there was a full gathering
of her guests round the tea-table on this particular afternoon. And,
in spite of the blankness of the season and the triteness of the occa-

sion, there was no trace in the company of that fatigued restlessness which means a dread of the pianola and a subdued hankering for auction bridge. The undisguised open-mouthed attention of the entire party was fixed on the homely negative personality of Mr Cornelius Appin. Of all her guests, he was the one who had come to Lady Blemley with the vaguest reputation. Someone had said he was "clever", and he had got his invitation in the moderate expectation, on the part of his hostess, that some portion at least of his cleverness would be contributed to the general entertainment. Until tea-time that day she had been unable to discover in what direction, if any, his cleverness lay. He was neither a wit nor a croquet champion, a hypnotic force nor a begetter of amateur theatricals. Neither did his exterior suggest the sort of man in whom women are willing to pardon a generous measure of mental deficiency. He had subsided into mere Mr Appin, and the Cornelius seemed a piece of transparent baptismal bluff. And now he was claiming to have launched on the world a discovery beside which the invention of gunpowder, of the printing press, and of steam locomotion were inconsiderable trifles. Science had made bewildering strides in many directions during recent decades, but this thing seemed to belong to the domain of the miracle rather than to scientific achievement.

"And do you really ask us to believe," Sir Wilfred was saying, "that you have discovered a means for instructing animals in the art of human speech and that dear old Tobermory has proved your first successful pupil?"

"It is a problem at which I have worked for the last seventeen years," said Mr Appin, "but only during the last eight or nine months have I been rewarded with glimmerings of success. Of course I have experimented with thousands of animals, but latterly only with cats, those wonderful creatures which have assimilated themselves so marvellously with our civilization while retaining all their highly developed feral instincts. Here and there among cats one comes across an outstanding superior intellect, just as one does among the ruck of human beings, and when I made the acquaintance of Tobermory a week ago I saw at once that I was in contact with a 'Beyond-cat' of extraordinary intelligence. I had gone far along the road to success in recent experiments; with Tobermory, as you call him, I have reached the goal."

Mr Appin concluded his remarkable statement in a voice which he strove to divest of a triumphant infection. No one said "Rats", though Clovis's lips moved in a monosyllabic contortion which probably invoked those rodents of disbelief.

"And do you mean to say," asked Miss Resker, after a slight pause, "that you have taught Tobermory to say and understand easy sentences of one syllable?"

"My dear Miss Resker," said the wonder-worker patiently, "one teaches little children and savages and backward adults in that piecemeal fashion; when one has solved the problem of making a beginning with an animal of highly developed intelligence one has no need for those halting methods. Tobermory can speak our language with perfect correctness."

This time Clovis very distinctly said, "Beyond-rats!" Sir Wilfred was more polite, but equally sceptical.

"Hadn't we better have the cat in and judge for ourselves?" suggested Lady Blemley.

Sir Wilfred went in search of the animal, and the company settled themselves down to the languid expectation of witnessing some more or less adroit drawing-room ventriloquism.

In a minute Sir Wilfred was back in the room, his face white beneath its tan and eyes dilated with excitement.

"By gad, it's true!"

His agitation was unmistakably genuine, and his hearers started forward in a thrill of awakened interest.

Collapsing into an armchair he continued breathlessly: "I found him dozing in the smoking-room, and called out to him to come for his tea. He blinked at me in his usual way, and I said, 'Come on, Toby; don't keep us waiting'; and, by Gad! he drawled out in a most horribly natural voice that he'd come when he dashed well pleased! I nearly jumped out of my skin!"

Appin had preached to absolutely incredulous hearers; Sir Wilfred's statement carried instant conviction. A Babel-like chorus of startled exclamation arose, amid which the scientist sat mutely enjoying the first fruit of his stupendous discovery.

In the midst of the clamour Tobermory entered the room and made his way with velvet tread and studied unconcern across to the group seated round the tea-table.

A sudden hush of awkwardness and constraint fell upon the company. Somehow there seemed an element of embarrassment in addressing on equal terms a domestic cat of acknowledged mental ability.

"Will you have some milk, Tobermory?" asked Lady Blemley in a rather strained voice.

"I don't mind if I do," was the response, couched in a tone of even indifference. A shiver of surpressed excitement went through the listeners, and Lady Blemley might be excused for pouring out the saucerful of milk rather unsteadily.

"I'm afraid I've spilt a good deal of it," she said apologetically.

"After all, it's not my Axminster," was Tobermory's rejoinder.

Another silence fell on the group, and then Miss Resker, in her best district-visitor manner, asked if the human language had been difficult to learn. Tobermory looked squarely at her for a moment and then fixed his gaze serenely on the middle distance. It was obvious that boring questions lay outside his scheme of life.

"What do you think of human intelligence?" asked Mavis Pellington lamely.

"Of whose intelligence in particular?" asked Tobermory coldly.

"Oh, well, mine for instance," said Mavis, with a feeble laugh.

"You put me in an embarrassing position," said Tobermory, whose tone and attitude certainly did not suggest a shred of embarrassment.

"When your inclusion in this house-party was suggested Sir Wilfred protested that you were the most brainless woman of his acquaintance, and that there was a broad distinction between hospitality and the care of the feeble-minded. Lady Blemley replied that your lack of brain-power was the precise quality which had earned you your invitation, as you were the only person she could think of who might be idiotic enough to buy their old car. You know, the one they call 'The Envy of Sisyphus', because it goes quite nicely uphill if you push it."

Lady Blemley's protestations would have had greater effect if she

had not casually suggested to Mavis only that morning that the car
in question would be just the thing for her down at her Devonshire
home.

Major Barfield plunged in heavily to effect a diversion.

"How about your carryings-on with the tortoiseshell puss up at
the stables, eh?"

The moment he had said it everyone realized the blunder.

"One does not usually discuss these matters in public," said
Tobermory frigidly. "From a slight observation of your ways since
you've been in this house I should imagine you'd find it incon-
venient if I were to shift the conversation on to your own little
affairs."

The panic which ensued was not confined to the major.

"Would you like to go and see if cook has got your dinner
ready?" suggested Lady Blemley hurriedly, affecting to ignore the
fact that it wanted at least two hours to Tobermory's dinner-time.

"Thanks," said Tobermory, "not quite so soon after my tea. I
don't want to die of indigestion."

"Cats have nine lives, you know," said Sir Wilfred heartily.

"Possibly," answered Tobermory; "but only one liver."

"Adelaide!" said Mrs Cornett, "do you mean to encourage that
cat to go out and gossip about us in the servants' hall?"

The panic had indeed become general. A narrow ornamental
balustrade ran in front of most of the bedroom windows at the
Towers, and it was recalled with dismay that this had formed a
favourite promenade for Tobermory at all hours, whence he could
watch the pigeons—and heaven knew what else besides. If he intended to become reminiscent in his present outspoken strain the
effect would be something more than disconcerting. Mrs Cornett,
who spent much time at her toilet table, and whose complexion was
reputed to be of a nomadic though punctual disposition, looked as
ill at ease as the Major. Miss Scrawen, who wrote fiercely sensuous
poetry and led a blameless life, merely displayed irritation; if you
are methodical and virtuous in private you don't necessarily want
everyone to know it. Bertie van Tahn, who was so depraved at
seventeen that he had long ago given up trying to be any worse,
turned a dull shade of gardenia white, but he did not commit the

error of dashing out of the room like Odo Finsberry, a young gentleman who was understood to be reading for the Church and who was possibly disturbed at the thought of scandals he might hear concerning other people. Clovis had the presence of mind to maintain a composed exterior; privately he was calculating how long it would take to procure a box of fancy mice through the agency of the *Exchange and Mart* as a species of hush-money.

Even in a delicate situation like the present, Agnes Resker could not endure to remain too long in the background.

"Why did I ever come down here?" she asked dramatically.

Tobermory immediately accepted the opening.

"Judging by what you said to Mrs Cornett on the croquet-lawn yesterday, you were out for food. You described the Blemleys as the dullest people to stay with that you knew, but said they were clever enough to employ a first-rate cook; otherwise they'd find it difficult to get anyone to come down a second time."

"There's not a word of truth in it! I appeal to Mrs Cornett—" exclaimed the discomfited Agnes.

"Mrs Cornett repeated your remark afterwards to Bertie van Tahn," continued Tobermory, and said, "That woman is a regular Hunger Marcher; she'd go anywhere for four square meals a day," and Bertie van Tahn said—"

At this point the chronicle mercifully ceased. Tobermory had caught a glimpse of the big yellow Tom from the Rectory working his way through the shrubbery towards the stable wing. In a flash he had vanished through the open French window.

With the disappearance of his too brilliant pupil Cornelius Appin found himself beset by a hurricane of bitter upbraiding, anxious enquiry, and frightened entreaty. The responsibility for the situation lay with him, and he must prevent matters from becoming worse. Could Tobermory impart his dangerous gift to other cats? was the first question he had to answer. It was possible, he replied, that he might have initiated his intimate friend the stable puss into his new accomplishment, but it was unlikely that his teaching could have taken a wider range as yet.

"Then," said Mrs Cornett, "Tobermory may be a valuable cat

and a great pet; but I'm sure you'll agree, Adelaide, that both he and the stable cat must be done away with without delay."

"You don't suppose I've enjoyed the last quarter of an hour, do you?" said Lady Blemley bitterly. "My husband and I are very fond of Tobermory—at least, we were before this horrible accomplishment was infused into him; but now, of course, the only thing is to have him destroyed as soon as possible."

"We can put some strychnine in the scraps he always gets at dinner-time," said Sir Wilfred, "and I will go and drown the stable cat myself. The coachman will be very sore at losing his pet, but I'll say a very catching form of mange has broken out in both cats and we're afraid of it spreading to the kennels."

"But my great discovery!" expostulated Mr Appin; "after all my years of research and experiment—"

"You can go and experiment on the short-horns at the farm, who are under proper control," said Mrs Cornett, "or the elephants at the Zoological Gardens. They're said to be highly intelligent, and they have this recommendation, that they don't come creeping about our bedrooms and under chairs, and so forth."

An archangel ecstatically proclaiming the Millenium, and then finding that it clashed unpardonably with Henley and would have to be indefinitely postponed, could hardly have felt more crestfallen than Cornelius Appin at the reception of his wonderful achievement. Public opinion, however, was against him—in fact, had the general voice been consulted on the matter it is probable that a strong minority would have been in favour of including him in the strychnine diet.

Defective train arrangements and a nervous desire to see matters brought to a finish prevented an immediate dispersal of the party, but dinner that evening was not a social success. Sir Wilfred had had rather a trying time with the stable cat and subsequently with the coachman. Agnes Resker ostentatiously limited her repast to a morsel of dry toast, which she bit as though it were a personal enemy; whilst Mavis Pellington maintained a vindictive silence throughout the meal. Lady Blemley kept up a flow of what she hoped was conversation, but her attention was fixed on the doorway. A plateful of carefully dosed fish scraps was in readiness on the sideboard, but sweets and savoury and dessert went their way, and no Tobermory appeared either in the dining-room or kitchen.

The sepulchral dinner was cheerful compared to the subsequent vigil in the smoking-room. Eating and drinking had at least supplied a distraction and cloak to the prevailing embarrassment. Bridge was out of the question in the general tension of nerves and tempers, and after Odo Finsberry had given a lugubrious rendering of "Melisande in the Wood" to a frigid audience, music was tacitly avoided. At eleven the servants went to bed, announcing that the small window in the pantry had been left open as usual for Tobermory's private use. The guests read steadily through the current batch of magazines, and fell back gradually on the "Badminton Library" and bound volumes of *Punch*. Lady Blemley made periodic visits to the pantry, returning each time with an expression of listless depression which forestalled questioning.

At two o'clock Clovis broke the dominating silence.

"He won't turn up tonight. He's probably in the local newspaper office at the present moment, dictating the first instalment of his reminiscences. Lady What's-her-name's book won't be in it. It will be the event of the day."

Having made this contribution to the general cheerfulness, Clovis went to bed. At long intervals the various members of the house-party followed his example.

The servants taking round the early tea made a uniform announcement to a uniform question. Tobermory had not returned.

Breakfast was, if anything, a more unpleasant function than dinner had been, but before its conclusion the situation was relieved. Tobermory's corpse was brought in from the shrubbery, where a gardener had just discovered it. From the bites on his throat and the yellow fur which coated his claws it was evident that he had fallen in unequal combat with the big Tom from the Rectory.

By midday most of the guests had quitted the Towers, and after lunch Lady Blemley had sufficiently recovered her spirits to write an extremely nasty letter to the Rectory about the loss of her valuable pet.

Tobermory had been Appin's one successful pupil, and he was destined to have no successor. A few weeks later an elephant in the

Dresden Zoological Garden, which had shown no previous signs of irritability, broke loose and killed an Englishman who had apparently been teasing it. The victim's name was variously reported in the papers as Oppin and Eppelin, but his front name was faithfully rendered Cornelius.

"If he was trying German irregular verbs on the poor beast," said Clovis, "he deserved all he got."

FLUFFY

by Theodore Sturgeon

PERSONALLY I BELIEVE *that Tobermory was much too clever to allow himself to be beaten by that vulgar yellow Tom. It's my theory that Tobermory engineered the whole thing, right down to the body of a cat that sufficiently resembled him for the ruse to work. Then he changed his name and set off to find a less dangerous situation where a cat of his quality would be accorded the respect due to him.*

In Fluffy, *Theodore Sturgeon seems to confirm my theory yet I doubt if the author was aware of the full implications when he wrote down Fluffy's story.*

For over thirty years now, Theodore Sturgeon has been producing first-rate stories of fantasy and science-fiction including a classic novel of a modern Vampire, Some of Your Blood. *Although he now seems to concentrate on writing for films and television, Mr. Sturgeon shows no signs of exhausting his remarkable imagination.*

Ransome lay in the dark and smiled to himself, thinking about his hostess. Ransome was always in demand as a house guest, purely because of his phenomenal abilities as a raconteur. Said abilities were entirely due to his being so often a house guest, for it was the terse beauty of his word pictures of people and their opinions of people that made him the figure he was and all those clipped ironies had to do with the people he had met last week-end. Staying a while at the Joneses, he could quietly insinuate the most scandalously hilarious things about the Joneses when he week-ended with the Browns the following fortnight. You think Mr and Mrs Jones

resented that? Ah, no. You should hear the dirt on the Browns!
And so it went, a two-dimensional spiral on the social plane.

This wasn't the Joneses or the Browns, though. This was Mrs
Benedetto's ménage; and to Ransome's somewhat jaded sense of
humour, the widow Benedetto was a godsend. She lived in a world
of her own, which was apparently set about with quasi-important
ancestors and relatives exactly as her living-room was cluttered up
with perfunctory unmentionable examples of Victorian rococo.

Mrs Benedetto did not live alone. Far from it. Her very life, to
paraphrase the lady herself, was wound about, was caught up in,
was owned by and dedicated to her baby. Her baby was her beloved,
her little beauty, her too darling my dear, and—so help me—her
boobly wutsi-wutsikins. In himself he was quite a character. He
answered to the name of Bubbles, which was inaccurate and offended
his dignity. He had been christened Fluffy, but you know how it is
with nicknames. He was large and he was sleek, that paragon among
animals, a chastened alley-rabbit.

Wonderful things, cats. A cat is the only animal which can live
like a parasite and maintain to the utmost its ability to take care of
itself. You've heard of little lost dogs, but you never heard of a lost
cat. Cats don't get lost, because cats don't belong anywhere. You
wouldn't get Mrs Benedetto to believe that. Mrs Benedetto never
thought of putting Fluffy's devotion to the test by declaring a ten-
day moratorium on the canned salmon. If she had, she would have
uncovered a sense of honour comparable with that of a bed-bug.

Knowing this—Ransome pardoned himself the pun—categoric-
ally, Ransome found himself vastly amused. Mrs Benedetto's
ministrations to the phlegmatic Fluffy were positively orgiastic.
As he thought of it in detail, he began to feel that perhaps, after
all, Fluffy was something of a feline phenomenon. A cat's ears are
sensitive organs; any living being that could abide Mrs Benedetto's
constant flow of conversation from dawn till dark, and then hear it
subside in sleep only to be replaced by a nightshift of resounding
snores; well, that *was* phenomenal. And Fluffy had stood it for four
years. Cats are not renowned for their patience. They have, however, a very fine sense of values. Fluffy was getting something out

of it—worth considerably more to him than the discomforts he
endured, too, for no cat likes to break even.

He lay still, marvelling at the carrying power of the widow's
snores. He knew little of the late Mr Benedetto, but he gathered
now that he had been either a man of saintly patience, a maso-
chist or a deaf-mute. A noise like that from just one stringy throat
must be an impossibility, and yet, there it was. Ransome liked to
imagine that the woman had calluses on her palate and tonsils,
grown there from her conversation, and it was these rasping
together that produced the curious dry-leather quality of her snores.
He tucked the idea away for future reference. He might use it next
week-end. The snores were hardly the gentlest of lullabies, but any
sound is soothing if it is repeated often enough.

There is an old story about a lighthouse tender whose lighthouse
was equipped with an automatic cannon which fired every fifteen
minutes, day and night. One night, when the old man was asleep,
the gun failed to go off. Three seconds after its stated time, the old
fellow was out of his bed and flailing around the room, shouting,
"What was that?" And so it was with Ransome.

He couldn't tell whether it was an hour after he had fallen asleep,
or whether he had not fallen asleep at all. But he found himself
sitting on the edge of the bed, wide awake, straining every nerve
for the source of the—what was it?—sound?—that had awakened
him. The old house was as quiet as a city morgue after closing time,
and he could see nothing in the tall, dark guest-room but the moon-
silvered windows and the thick blacknesses that were drapes. Any
old damn thing might be hiding behind those drapes, he thought
comfortingly. He edged himself back on the bed and quickly
snatched his feet off the floor. Not that anything was under the bed,
but still—

A white object puffed along the floor, through the moonbeams,
towards him. He made no sound, but tensed himself, ready to
attack or defend, dodge or retreat. Ransome was by no means an
admirable character, but he owed his reputation and therefore his
existence, to this particular trait, the ability to poise himself, in-
vulnerable to surprise. Try arguing with a man like that some time.

The white object paused to stare at him out of its yellow-green eyes. It was only Fluffy—Fluffy looking casual and easy-going and not at all in a mood to frighten people. In fact he looked up at Ransome's gradually relaxing bulk and raised a long-haired, quizzical eyebrow, as if he rather enjoyed the man's discomfiture.

Ransome withstood the cat's gaze with suavity, and stretched himself out on the bed with every bit of Fluffy's own easy grace. "Well," he said amusedly, "you gave me a jolt! Weren't you taught to knock before you entered a gentleman's boudoir?"

Fluffy raised a velvet paw and touched it pinkly with his tongue. "Do you take me for a barbarian?" he asked.

Ransome's lids seemed to get heavy, the only sign he ever gave of being taken aback. He didn't believe for a moment that the cat had really spoken, but there was something about the voice he had heard that was more than a little familiar. This was, of course, someone's idea of a joke!

Good God—it had to be a joke!

Well, he had to hear that voice again before he could place it. "You didn't say anything of course," he told the cat, "but if you did, what was it?"

"You heard me the first time," said the cat, and jumped up on the foot of his bed. Ransome inched back from the animal. "Yes," he said, "I—thought I did." Where on earth had he heard that voice before? "You know," he said, with an attempt at jocularity, "you should, under these circumstances, have written me a note before you knocked."

"I refuse to be burdened with the so-called social amenities," said Fluffy. His coat was spotlessly clean, and he looked like an advertising photograph for eiderdown, but he began to wash carefully. "I don't like you, Ransome."

"Thanks," chuckled Ransome, surprised. "I don't like you either."

"Why?" asked Fluffy.

Ransome told himself silently that he was damned. He had recognized the cat's voice, and it was a credit to his powers of observation that he had. It was his own voice. He held tight to a mind that would begin to reel on slight provocation, and, as usual when bemused, he flung out a smoke-screen of his own variety of glib chatter.

"Reasons for not liking you," he said, "are legion. They are all included in the one phrase—'you are a cat'."

"I have heard you say that at least twice before," said Fluffy, "except that you have now substituted 'cat' for 'woman'."

"Your attitude is offensive. Is any given truth any the less true for having been uttered more than once?"

"No," said the cat with equanimity. "But it is just that more clichéd."

Ransome laughed. "Quite aside from the fact that you can talk, I find you most refreshing. No one has ever criticized my particular variety of repartee before."

"No one was ever wise to you before," said the cat. "Why don't you like cats?"

A question like that was, to Ransome, the pressing of a button which released ordered phrases. "Cats," he said oratorically, "are without doubt the most self-centred, ungrateful, hypocritical creatures on this or any other earth. Spawned from a mésalliance between Lilith and Satan—"

Fluffy's eyes widened. "Ah! An antiquarian!" he whispered.

"—they have the worst traits of both. Their best qualities are their beauty of form and of motion, and even these breathe evil. Women are the ficklest of bipeds, but few women are as fickle as, by nature, any cat is. Cats are not true. They are impossibilities, as perfection is impossible. No other living creature moves with utterly perfect grace. Only the dead can so perfectly relax. And nothing— simply nothing at all—transcends a cat's incomparable insincerity."

Fluffy purred.

"Pussy! Sit-by-the-fire and sing!" spat Ransome. "Smiling up all toadying and yellow-eyed at the bearers of liver and salmon and catnip! Soft little puffball, bundle of joy, playing with a ball on a string; making children clap their soft hands to see you, while your mean little brain is viciously alight with the pictures your play calls up for you. Bite it to make it bleed; hold it till it all but throttles; lay it down and step about it daintily; prod it with a gentle silken paw until it moves again, and then pounce. Clasp it in your talons then, lift it, roll over with it, sink your cruel teeth into it while you pump out its guts with your hind feet. Ball on a string! Play-actor!"

Fluffy yawned. "To quote you, that is the prettiest piece of emotional claptrap that these old ears have ever heard. A triumph in studied spontaneity. A symphony in cynicism. A poem in perception. The unqualified—"

Ransome grunted.

He deeply resented this flamboyant theft of all his pet phrases, but his lip twitched nevertheless. The cat was indeed an observant animal.

"—epitome of understatement," Fluffy finished smoothly. "To listen to you, one would think that you would like to slaughter earth's felinity."

"I would," gritted Ransome.

"It would be a favour to us," said the cat. "We would keep ourselves vastly amused, eluding you and laughing at the effort it cost you. Humans lack imagination."

"Superior creature," said Ransome ironically, "why don't you do away with the human race, if you find us a bore?"

"You think we couldn't?" responded Fluffy. "We can out-think, outrun and outbreed your kind. But why should we? As long as you act as you have for these last few thousand years, feeding us, sheltering us and asking nothing from us but our presence for purposes of admiration—why then, you may remain here."

Ransome guffawed. "Nice of you! But listen—stop your bland discussion of the abstract and tell me some things I want to know. How can you talk, and why did you pick me to talk to?"

Fluffy settled himself. "I shall answer the question socratically. Socrates was a Greek, and so I shall begin with your last question. What do you do for a living?"

"Why I—I have some investments and a small capital, and the interest—" Ransome stopped, for the first time fumbling for words. Fluffy was nodding knowingly.

"All right, all right. Come clean. You can speak freely."

Ransome grinned. "Well, if you must know—and you seem to—

I am a practically permanent house guest. I have a considerable fund of stories and a flair for telling them; I look presentable and act as if I were a gentleman. I negotiate, at times, small loans—"

"A loan," said Fluffy authoritatively, "is something one intends to repay."

"We'll call them loans," said Ransome airily. "Also, at one time and another, I exact a reasonable fee for certain services rendered—"

"Blackmail," said the cat.

"Don't be crude. All in all, I find life a comfortable and engrossing thing."

"Q.E.D.," said Fluffy triumphantly. "You make your living being scintillant, beautiful to look at. So do I. You help nobody but yourself; you help yourself to anything you want. So do I. No one likes you except those you bleed; everyone admires and envies you. So with me. Get the point?"

"I think so. Cat, you draw a mean parallel. In other words, you consider my behaviour catlike."

"Precisely," said Fluffy through his whiskers. "And that is both why and how I can talk with you. You're so close to the feline in everything you do and think; your whole basic philosophy is that of a cat. You have a feline aura about you so intense that it contacts mine; hence we find each other intelligible."

"I don't understand that," said Ransome.

"Neither do I," returned Fluffy. "But there it is. Do you like Mrs Benedetto?"

"No!" said Ransome immediately and with considerable emphasis. "She is absolutely insufferable. She bores me. She irritates me. She is the only woman in the world who can do both those things to me at the same time. She talks too much. She reads too little. She thinks not at all. Her mind is hysterically hidebound. She has a face like the cover of a book that no one has ever wanted to read. She is built like a pinch-type whisky bottle that never had any whisky in it. Her voice is monotonous and unmusical. Her education was insufficient. Her family background is mediocre, she can't cook, and she doesn't brush her teeth often enough."

"My, my," said the cat, raising both paws in surprise. "I detect a ring of sincerity in all that. It pleases me. That is exactly the way I have felt for some years. I have never found fault with her cooking, though; she buys special food for me. I am tired of it. I am tired of her. I am tired of her to an almost unbelievable extent. Almost as much as I hate you."

"Me?"

"Of course. You're an imitation. You're a phony. Your birth is against you, Ransome. No animal that sweats and shaves, that opens doors for women, that dresses itself in equally phony imitations of the skins of animals, can achieve the status of a cat. You are presumptuous."

"You're not?"

"I am different. I am a cat, and have a right to do as I please. I disliked you so intensely when I saw you this evening that I made up my mind to kill you."

"Why didn't you? Why—don't you?"

"I couldn't," said the cat coolly. "Not when you sleep like a cat . . . no, I thought of something far more amusing."

"Oh?"

"Oh yes." Fluffy stretched out a foreleg, extended his claws. Ransome noticed subconsciously how long and strong they seemed. The moon had gone its way, and the room was filled with slate-grey light.

"What woke you," said the cat, leaping to the window-sill, "just before I came in?"

"I don't know," said Ransome. "Some little noise, I imagine."

"No indeed," said Fluffy, curling his tail and grinning through his whiskers. "It was the stopping of a noise. Notice how quiet it is?"

It was indeed. There wasn't a sound in the house—oh yes, now he could hear the plodding footsteps of the maid on her way from the kitchen to Mrs Benedetto's bedroom, and the soft clink of a teacup. But otherwise—suddenly he had it. "The old horse stopped snoring!"

"She did," said the cat. The door across the hall opened, there was the murmur of the maid's voice, a loud crash, the most horrible scream Ransome had ever heard, pounding footsteps rushing down the hall, a more distant scream, silence. Ransome bounced out of bed. "What the hell—"

"Just the maid," said Fluffy, washing between his toes, but keeping the corners of his eyes on Ransome. "She just found Mrs Benedetto."

"Found—"

"Yes. I tore her throat out."

"Good—God! Why?"

Fluffy poised himself on the window-sill. "So you'd be blamed for it," he said, and laughing nastily, he leaped out and disappeared in the grey morning.

CAT AND MOUSE

by Ramsey Campbell

T H E I D E A F O R *this anthology first came to me some years ago when I was still at school. In fact, I can remember drawing up a list of possible stories in class, from behind the cover of a third form maths textbook. At the time I wrote to another schoolboy, an aspiring author, asking for a suitable story. He politely pointed out that I lacked the wherewithal to finance such an ambitious project.*

Now still only in his twenties, that aspiring author has established himself a reputation as one of England's leading weird-story writers with two collections of short stories to his credit, The Inhabitant of the Lake *and* Demons by Daylight, *as well as numerous anthology and magazine contributions. It seems only fitting that I should here include a story by Ramsey Campbell and* Cat and Mouse *is amongst his very best.*

You couldn't say that the house crouched. Yet as we came off the roundabout on whose edge the house stood, and stooped beneath the trees which hung glistening over the garden, I had an impression of stealth. It couldn't be related to anything; not the summer glare nor the white house within the garden. But silence settled on us, and the circling cars hushed. And although the sunlight glittered on the last raindrops dripping from the leaves, a waiting shadow touched us and the quiet in the garden seemed poised to leap.

I had to struggle with the key in the unfamiliar lock; my wife Hazel laughed, annoying me a little. I'd wanted to throw the door wide and carry her in, enjoying my triumph; God knows I'd gone through enough to buy the house. But at least I enjoyed her delight once I managed to open the door.

We'd seen the house before, of course, when we were furnishing the rooms, but now we both felt a shock of unfamiliarity. The white telephone amazed us; so did the stairs, a construction of treads like the tail of a kite which was the major addition we owed to the previous tenants. Hazel's was the reaction I could have predicted; she rushed through the downstairs rooms and then clattered upstairs, eager to own the rest of the house. As I watched her run up the open stairs I felt a dull surge of desire. But when I made my own tour of the pale green living-room, the white kitchen cold as a hospital, the bathroom with its abstract blocks of colour and its pink pedestal, I felt imprisoned. The air smelt slightly dank, like fur. Of course Hazel had been wearing her sheepskin coat, but it seemed odd that the entire ground floor should smell of wet fur, a smell that trailed with me like a cloak. I began to open windows. Perhaps, since we'd lived on a third floor for years, I simply needed time to adjust to entering a house whose windows weren't open.

I found Hazel within a maze of double-jointed lights and drawing-board and cartons of books, in the room we'd decided to use as an attic. The smell was stronger here. "Come down and I'll make some tea," she said.

"Just let me tidy up a little."

"You've done enough for a while, love."

"You mean selling myself?" I said, thinking of my ideas and my art which I'd battered against the advertising agency where I worked until they had been battered half out of shape.

"No, I mean selling your talent," Hazel said, then with an edge of doubt: "You do like our house, don't you?"

"Of course I do. That's why I worked to buy it," I said and stopped, peering down at the windowsill. We had liked the rough wood of that sill, and had left it unpainted. But now, trying to peer closer without appearing to do so, I saw that the sill looked chewed. Or clawed. The former owners must have had a cat or a dog. That was the explanation, yet I was disturbed to think that they had locked it in here, for nothing else could have driven it to such a frenzy that it would have left its claw-marks on the sill and even in the putty round the window-pane.

"I'm sure you'll sleep now that we're here," Hazel said, and I started. "What are you looking so worried about?" she said.

I was thinking how, when I'd stripped the attic to paint it, I had noticed claw-marks tearing through the wallpaper without realizing until now what they were, but I didn't want to upset her; besides, I wished she wouldn't probe me so often, even though it was out of love she did so. "I'm wondering where the stereo is," I said.

"It must be on its way," she said. "They'll take care of it. They can see how expensive it is."

"Yes, well," I told her, faintly annoyed that I should feel bound to explain this point again, "it's the most sensitive. You have to pay for sensitivity."

"I know you do," she said smiling, and I realized she'd found another meaning, a personal meaning which she wanted to share with me. Sometimes her insistence on puns infuriated me; often it made me love her more. I coaxed my gaze away from the patch on the wall where the paper had been clawed. "I wouldn't mind dinner," I said.

The stereo arrived after dinner, halfway through my third cup of coffee. The workmen were clearly annoyed that I should supervise them, as if I were showing them how to do their job. But it was only a job to them; to me it was perfection in jeopardy. When they'd left I played *Ein Heldenleben* at full volume, caring nothing for the neighbours, since they were beyond the garden. Hazel listened quietly, more in order not to disturb me than out of a genuine response to the music. Somehow I felt trapped, the Strauss surged against Hazel's tranquil uncommunicative face, against the padded silence of the room, and never broke. I crossed to the windows and flung them high, and the feeling streamed out into the dark garden, where its remnants clung to the trees.

That night I could neither make love nor sleep. Outside the bedroom window cars whirred lingeringly by, like a sound by Stockhausen passing across speakers. My wife slept buried in the pillow, frowning, her thumb in her mouth. The tip of my cigarette glowed and reddened the landing; it opened in the gloss of the doors like a crimson eye, watching from the attic and from the other bedroom whose purpose was beginning to seem increasingly futile. I had meant to go downstairs, but down there or in my ears lay a faint ominous hiss, quite unlike the threshing of the leaves above the garden. I listened for a few minutes, then I scraped my cigarette on the ashtray by the bed and pulled the covers up.

Hazel woke me at noon. I gathered she'd awoken only recently herself. I unstuck myself from sleep and followed her downstairs. I must have looked disgruntled, judging by Hazel's glances at me. I felt she'd woken me up merely for company. When we reached the living-room she said: "Darling, listen."

I heard only the words, which were the formula she used when she wasn't sure that I would agree. Of course her tone implied another meaning, but I wasn't awake enough to notice. "What is it?" I demanded.

"No, *listen*."

That was the second half of the formula. I often spent an hour before sleep juggling ideas and an hour after breakfast waking up; nothing angers me more than to be called upon to make a decision before I'm awake. "Look," I said, "for Christ's sake, now that you've dragged me out of bed—"

Then I saw that she had been gazing at the stereo. From its speakers came a sound like the hiss of a hostile audience.

"You see, it moves back and forth," Hazel said. "The stereo must have been on all night. Will it have gone wrong?"

"I take it you've left it on to make sure it will?" I couldn't tell her that I wasn't shouting at her but at something else, because I didn't care to admit it to myself. But as I pulled out *Ein Heldenleben* and almost ripped it with the stylus I felt the movement of the hiss, felt it loom like a lurking predator, an actual dark physical presence, as it crept from one speaker to another. Then the Strauss rushed richly out. It sounded perfect, but aside from that it meant nothing. I took it off, scowled at Hazel and stumped back to bed.

I was running upstairs, and the stairs tilted steeply like a ladder. Suddenly sliding gates clanged shut at both ends of the staircase, and something groped hugely through the wall and felt around the trap for me. I awoke struggling. The blanket lay heavy and fluid on my body like a cat, and my skin prickled with what felt like the memory of claws. I threw off the blanket and sat up.

For a moment I was lost; I stared at the blue walls, the grey wall, the impossible silence. I struggled to my feet and listened. It was five o'clock, and there should have been more sound; Hazel should have been audible; the silence seemed charged, alert, on tiptoe. I made my way downstairs, padding carefully. I didn't know what I might find.

Hazel was sitting in the living-room, a book in her hand. I couldn't tell whether she'd been crying; her face looked scrubbed as it would have if she had wept, but I was confused by the thought that this might be the impression she had contrived for me. More disturbingly I felt that something had happened to change the silence while I had been asleep.

She came to the end of a chapter and inserted a bookmark. "I like to sleep too, you know," she said.

"No doubt," I said, and that was that. Through dinner we didn't speak, we hardly looked at each other. It was less that each of us was waiting for the other to speak than as if the silence itself was poised to pounce on the first to succumb. Several times I was almost frightened enough to speak, so that at least my fears might be defined; but each time I determined that it was up to Hazel to begin.

I don't know what music I played after dinner; I recall only visualizing fists of sound crudely battling the blankets of silence. I looked at Hazel, who was trying to read against the barrage of noise which for the moment had lost all meaning. I felt grief for what I might be beginning to destroy. "I'm sorry," I said. "Maybe I'm starting to crack up."

Sometimes Hazel would dodge around the bedroom and I, having pinned her to the bed, would rape her; we seemed to need this more and more often. But tonight we waltzed gently over each other, exploring delicately, until I was too deep in her to need ornamentations. "You're a deep one," I said.

"What, love?" she gasped, laughing.

But I could never offer her puns more than once, and now less than ever, for my body had stiffened and chilled. Perhaps, despite her reassurances, I was cracking up. I knew that at that moment I was being watched. I peered down into Hazel's eyes and tried to gaze through them, and as I felt her nails move on my back I remembered the sensations of claws at the end of my dream.

The next day, Monday, I came home tired by a lunch which one of our clients had bought me; my constant smile had felt more like a death-grin, and certainly had expressed as little emotion. Returning to the agency I'd walked through shafts of envy which had penetrated even my six whiskies. Our house should have offered peace, but all I felt as I opened the front door was the taut snap of tension. I felt awaited, and not only by Hazel.

In the early evening cars passed with a muffled undulating hum, but soon faded. I remembered that back at our flat we could always hear the plop of a tap like a dropper or the echoing cries of children in the baths across the road. Here in the house the silence seemed worse than ever, threatening to drown us, and our speech was waterlogged. Yet it wasn't the silence I found most distrubing. Over dinner and afterwards, as we sat reading, I glimpsed an odd expression several times on Hazel's face. It wasn't fear, exactly; I should have described it as closer to doubt. What upset me most was that each time she caught me watching her, she quickly smiled.

I couldn't stop thinking that something had happened while I had been at work. "How was our house today?" I asked.

"It was fine," she said. "Oh, while I was out shopping—"

But I wouldn't let her escape. "Do you like our house, then?" I asked.

"What do you think?"

I was certain now that she was hiding something from me, but I didn't know how to find it. She could elude my questions by any number of wiles, by weeping if necessary. Frowning, I desisted and put Britten's *Curlew River* on the stereo. Of all Britten's work I love the church parables more than any; their sureness and astringency can make me forget my crumpled colleagues at the agency and their clumsy machinations. I thought *Curlew River* might help me define my thoughts. But I didn't get as far as the second side, with its angelic resolution. Peter Pears' eerie vocal glissandi in the part of the madwoman chilled me like the howls of a sad cat; the church which the stereo re-created seemed longer and more hollow, like a tunnel gaping invisibly before me in the air. And the calm silences with which Britten punctuates his parables seemed no longer calm. They seemed to pounce closer and to grow as they approached Determined to respond to the music, I closed my eyes. At once I felt a dark stealthy shape leap at me between the music. My eyes started open, and I glanced to Hazel for some kind of support. The room was empty.

And it was dark. On the wall opposite me the wallpaper hung clawed into strips. It was not the living-room. Perhaps I cried out, for I heard Hazel call "Don't worry, you're all right," and something else inaudible. I saw that the wallpaper was after all not clawed, that it was merely shadows that had made it seem so. Then Hazel came in with a tray.

"What did you say?" I demanded.

"Nothing," she said. "I crept out to make some coffee."

"Just now, I mean. When you called out."

"I haven't said a word for ten minutes," she said.

After Hazel had gone to bed I stayed downstairs for an hour of last cigarettes and fragments of slogans. The month looked slack at the agency, but I couldn't stop thinking, and I preferred not to think about the house. Eventually, of course, the house overtook my thoughts. All right, I argued in mute fury, if I were moved by Britten's melodious angels then I might as well admit to a lurking belief in the supernatural. So the house was haunted by the presence of a dog or, as I sensed intuitively, a cat: so what? It didn't worry me, and Hazel hadn't even noticed. But if my grudging belief was the latest fashion in enlightenment, the retreat from scepticism, it didn't seem to be helping me. Spectral cats could have nothing to do with my hearing Hazel's voice when she hadn't spoken. I felt that my mind was beginning to fray.

A paroxysm of dry coughs persuaded me to stub out my cigarette. I threw the scribbled scraps of paper into the fireplace and came out into the hall. As I turned out the light in the living-room, a shadow leapt from the hall to the landing with a single bound.

Of course I wasn't sure, and I tried to be less so. I crept upstairs, feeling my heels hang over the open treads of the staircase. For a moment my nightmare returned, and I was heaving myself up a tilted ladder which grew steeper as the gaps between the treads widened. Halfway up I could hear myself panting with exhaustion, perhaps from lack of sleep. At the top the shadows crowded indistinguishably. On tiptoe, I opened the bedroom door. I had drawn it back only inches when a fluid shadow rippled through the crack into the room.

I threw the door open, and Hazel jumped. I was certain she had, although it might have been the bedroom light jarring her blanketed shape into focus. As I undressed I watched her, and after a minute or two she shifted a little. Now I was convinced that she hadn't been asleep when I entered, and was still only pretending. I didn't try to make sure, but it took me some time to turn out the light and slip into bed. For minutes I stood staring at Hazel's obscured body, wondering where the shadow had gone.

I awoke feeling lightened. The room gave out its colours brilliantly; beyond the window waves of leaves sprang up glowing in the sun. It was only as sleep began to peel back a little that I wondered whether Hazel's absence had lightened me.

Once downstairs I didn't go to her. Instead I walked dully into the dark living-room and slumped on the settee. I began to wonder whether I was afraid of Hazel. Certainly I couldn't talk to her about last night. My eyes began to close, and the living-room darkened further. Shadows striped the wall again; in a moment the wallpaper might peel. Or a claw might tear through—The door gushed light and Hazel came in, carrying plates of breakfast. She smiled when I leapt to my feet, but I wasn't greeting her. The living-room was bright, as it had been since I'd entered. I had realized whom I might see. After all, the house was his responsibility.

"How do you feel?" I said, staring into my coffee then glancing up at her.

"All right, love. Don't start worrying about me. I should try and have a rest today if I were you."

I didn't know whether the shadow was speaking; in any case, I resented the implication that I looked incapable. "I'm going to take a couple of hours off this morning," I said. "If you want to come— I mean, if you want to get away from the house for a while—"

"Silly," she said. "You'd be upset if dinner wasn't ready."

My suspicions were confirmed. I couldn't believe that she wouldn't take the chance to escape the house unless it had infected her somehow. I was glad that I hadn't told her where I was going. I managed to kiss her, forgetting to notice whether the feel of her had changed, and hurried round the corner to the car. Muffled thunder hung in the air. For a moment I regretted leaving Hazel alone, but I was afraid to return to the house. Besides, perhaps she was past rescuing. I drove blindly around the roundabout, not looking at the house, and was at the estate agent's within half an hour.

I had forgotten that the office wouldn't be open. I had a cup of coffee and a few cigarettes in a café across the road, and by the time the estate agent arrived I had perfected my smile and my story. A faint astringent scent clung to him, and he pulled at his silver moustache more often than when first I'd met him. I convinced him that I had merely been passing, but still he drew his rings nervously from his fingers and paced behind his desk. At last I fastened on the shrill garrulous couple who had been leaving as I entered, and guided the conversation to them.

"Yes, abominable," he agreed. "I suppose I dislike people. I decided to live with cats a long time ago. People and dogs can be led where cats can't. You'd never train a cat to salivate at your whim."

"Were there cats in our house?" I said.

"Have you been dreaming?" he demanded.

"Just a feeling."

"You're right, of course," he said. "To me, you know, the most frightful act is to kill or maim a cat. Don't offer me Auschwitz. People aren't beautiful. Auschwitz was unforgivable, but there's nothing worse than a man who destroys beauty."

"What happened?" I said, trying to be casual.

"I shan't go into detail," he said. "Briefly, your predecessors were obsessed with pests. One mouse and they were convinced the house was overrun. There are none there now, of course. People and cats have one thing in common: they can lose themselves in their own internal drives to the exclusion of morality, or reality for that matter."

"Go on," I said.

"Well, these people left five cats in the house without food while they went away on holiday. Starve a cat to kill a mouse, you see— as stupid and vile as that. Somehow the attic door closed and trapped the cats. When our friends returned they opened the front door and one cat ran out, never to be seen again. The others were in pieces in the attic. Cannibalism."

"And no doubt," I said, "if someone exceptionally sensitive were to take the house—"

"Yourself, you mean?"

"Yes, perhaps so," I said defensively. "Or for that matter, if one left some piece of sensitive electrical equipment running—"

"I don't pretend to know," he said, but there was despair around his eyes. "Ghosts of cats? I'll tell you this. People underrate the intelligence of cats simply because they refuse to be taught tricks. I think the ghosts of cats would play with their victims for a while, as revenge. Sometimes I wonder what I'm doing in this job," he said. "You can see I don't care."

When I left I drove slowly through the city, thinking. The lunch-time crowds eddied about me; eventually the thickening sky above the roofs was split by lightning, and grey rain leapt from the pavements, washing away the crowds. I drove on as the rain smashed at the windscreen. "Playing with their victims"—there was something to which that was the key. If I were to believe in ghosts, however absurd it seemed beneath the tic of traffic lights, I might as well accept the idea of possession. Was the house playing us as hunter and victim? But I couldn't altogether believe that one's personality could be ousted; I could imagine a framework within which this might be logical, but I wasn't sure that I felt it to be real. Yet I noticed that here, caged in by ropes of rain, I still felt more free than recently: free of the house's influence.

Suddenly I wanted to be with Hazel. If I had to I would drag her out, whatever was within her, however dangerous she might be. I could telephone my agency when I arrived at the house. I turned my car and it coursed through the pools of the city.

Along the carriageways out of the city the trees looked bedraggled and broken. Occasionally I passed torn cars, steaming where they'd skidded in mud. I was hardly surprised, when I reached the house, to see that the telephone wire had snapped and was sagging between the roof and the trees in the garden. As I drove past the roundabout it occurred to me that if Hazel were a victim she was trapped now. She would have to admit that she was as vulnerable as me. No longer would I have to suffer the entire burden of disquiet.

I think it was not until I got out of the car that I perceived what I had been thinking. I felt a chill of horror at myself. I loved her hands on my back, yet for a while I had turned them into claws. All along Hazel had been frightened but had tried to hide her fear from me. That was the doubt that I'd seen in her eyes. At once I knew what had blinded me, what had sought to destroy her. The rain dwindled and the sun blazed out; a rainbow lifted above the carriageway. I rushed through the garden, lashed by wet leaves, and dragged open the door to the house.

The house was dark—darker than it should have been now that the sun had returned. It was dim with stealth and silence. There was no sound of Hazel. I hurried through the ground floor, stumbled upstairs and searched the bedrooms, but the house seemed empty. I gazed down from the landing and saw that the front door was still open. I was ready to run out and wait for Hazel outside, yet I couldn't rid myself of the impression that the staircase was far longer and steeper than I remembered. Trying to control my fears I started down. I was halfway down when a shadow crept across the carpet in the living-room.

For a moment I thought it was Hazel's. But not only did its shape relate to something else entirely—it was far too large. I stood on the edge of the stairs. If I ran now, whatever was moving in the dim room might misjudge its leap. I wavered, fell down two stairs and jumped clumsily to the hall. At that moment the telephone rang.

In my terror I could see it only as an ally. I backed up the stairs, reached down and caught up the receiver. I muttered incoherently, then I heard Hazel's voice.

"I've got out," she said. "I hoped I might catch you before you came home. Is the door open?"

"Yes," I said. "Listen, love—don't come back in. I'm sorry. I didn't understand what was going on. I blamed you."

"If the door's open you can make it," she said. "Just run as fast as you can"—and then I remembered that the telephone wire was down, remembered the voice that had called to me from the other room.

As I dropped the receiver the air came alive with hissing. It was the sound that the stereo had trapped, but worse now, overpowering. I launched myself from the stairs and came down in the middle of the hall. One more leap and I would be outside. But before I regained my balance I had seen that the front door was closed.

I might have wasted my strength in trying to wrench it open. But although I didn't understand the rules of what was happening, I felt that if the house had tried to convince me that Hazel was safe that meant she was still inside somewhere. Behind me the hall spat. I clutched at the front door. I told myself that I was only using it for support, and turned.

It took me some time to determine where I was. In the dimness the hall seemed green, and a good deal smaller. I might have been in the living-room. But I wasn't, for I could see the stairs; the walls weren't closing like a trap; the shadows hadn't massed into a poised shape, ready to sink its claws into my back. My mind began to scream and scrabble at itself, and I concentrated on the stairs. Eventually, after some hours, the hall imperceptibly altered and seemed stretched to dim infinity. The stairs were miles away. It wasn't worth making for them. There was an acre of open space to be crossed, and I knew I had no chance.

I cried out for Hazel, and from somewhere above she answered my cry.

That cry I knew wasn't faked. It was scarcely coherent, pulled out of shape by terror; it was scarcely Hazel, and in some way I knew that guaranteed its truth. I ran to the stairs, counting my foot-steps. Two, and I was on the stairs. I had control of the situation for a moment. I should have kept going blindly; I shouldn't have looked round. But I couldn't help glancing into the living-room.

The doorway was dark, and in the darkness a face appeared, flashed and was gone, like the momentary luminous spectres in a ghost train. I glimpsed an enormous black head, glowing green eyes, a red mouth barred with white teeth. Then I tore my gaze away and looked up to the landing, and I saw that the stairs had become a towering ladder, a succession of great treads separated by yawning gaps which I could never cross. The air hissed behind me, and I could go neither up nor down.

Then Hazel cried out again. There was only one way to conquer myself, and my mind was so numbed that I managed it. I shut my eyes tight and crawled upwards, grasping each higher stair and dragging myself painfully over space. Beneath me I felt the stairs tremble. I wondered whether they would throw me off, until I realized that something was climbing up behind me. I tightened every muscle of my face to keep my brain from bursting out, and heaved myself upward. I felt a purring breath on my neck, and then I was on the landing.

I stumbled to my feet and opened my eyes. Unless the house was able to blot Hazel from my gaze, she could only be in the one room I hadn't searched, the attic. As I ran across the landing, a huge face flashed at the top of the stairs. Its eyes gleamed with bottom-less hatred, and for a second it seemed to fill with teeth. Then I had reached the attic and slammed the door.

I slumped. The attic was so crowded with lamps and cartons that nobody could have hidden there. The objects massed, suffocated and strung together by cords of dust; I didn't see how I could even make my way between them. I might be trapped in the maze and cut off from Hazel, if indeed she were in the room. I knocked one of the looming cartons to the floor in an attempt to clear the view, and on the thud of the carton I heard breath hiss in muffled terror.

At once the room rearranged itself, and I saw Hazel. She was crouched in a corner, her knees drawn up to her chin, her arms pressed tight over her face. She was sobbing. I moved gently

towards her, loving her, bullying the fear from my mind. My feet
tangled in wire. I looked down and saw the cord for the lamps. I
knew where the socket was; I plugged in the lamps and let them
blind the door. Then I went to Hazel.

"Come on, love," I said. "Come on, Hazel. We're going now.
Come on, love."

Her arms drew back from her face. She looked up at me; then she
shrank into the corner and her eyes gaped in horror. I fell back.
But her lips moved. She was trying to speak to me. She wasn't
frightened of me. I looked behind me, towards the door.

The door had opened, and the doorway was half-filled by an
enormous face. Its mouth yawned wide and a tongue sprang dripping across its teeth. I grabbed the lamps and shone them into its
eyes, but they didn't blink. Its face began to bulge in through the
doorway, and behind it others leapt across the landing to hover
grinning above the first. With a surge of pure energy and terror I
hurled the lamps at the faces.

What happened I don't know. I never heard the lamps strike the
floor. But the surge of energy carried me across the room to heave
the window open. I ran to Hazel and pulled her to her feet, although
she shrank sobbing into the corner. I threw her across my shoulder
and staggered with her to the window. I glanced back into the
room, where faces with gleaming eyes capered in the air and flew
at us in a single toothed mass. Then I jumped.

I think the house must have overlooked that. Mice might fall
from a window, but they aren't supposed to jump. So I spent time
in hospital with a broken leg, while Hazel was furious enough by the
end of the week to visit the estate agent's. Once she had made him
admit that he wouldn't spend a night in the house, the rest was
easy. "I have no time for horror," he told her. My leg soon im-
proved. Not so Hazel's insomnia; and yet when we lie awake
together talking through the uneasy hours, I think there are times
when we're grateful. Somehow we could never talk that way before.

THE CATS OF ULTHAR

by H. P. Lovecraft

LIKE POE BEFORE *him, Howard Phillips Lovecraft (1890–1937) was an ardent admirer of the Cat or, as Lovecraft put it, "the cool, lithe, cynical and unconquered lord of the housetops".*

A shy, retiring, almost recluse-like individual of archaic manners, this great American writer of the macabre seems to have taken greater pleasure in the company of Cats than of humans. He wrote poems on the death of favourite felines and once penned an effusive essay demonstrating the unquestionable superiority of the lordly Cat over the coarse canine.

Lovecraft's notes reveal that he planned to write at least three more stories in which Cats played a malevolent part. Unfortunately, these ideas remained undeveloped at the time of his death. The following brief tale is the only Lovecraft story to deal exclusively *with Cats.*

It is said that in Ulthar, which lies beyond the river Skai, no man may kill a cat; and this I can verily believe as I gaze upon him who sitteth purring before the fire. For the cat is cryptic, and close to strange things which men cannot see. He is the soul of antique Aegyptus, and bearer of tales from forgotten cites in Meroe and Ophir. He is the kin of the jungle's lords and heir to the secrets of hoary and sinister Africa. The Sphinx is his cousin, and he speaks her language; but he is more ancient than the Sphinx, and remembers that which she hath forgotten.

In Ulthar, before ever the burgesses forbade the killing of cats, there dwelt an old cotter and his wife who delighted to trap and slay cats of their neighbours. Why they did this I do not know; save that many hate the voice of the cat in the night, and take it ill that cats should run stealthily about yards and gardens at twilight. But whatever the reason, this old man and woman took pleasure in trapping and slaying every cat which came near to their hovel; and from some of the sounds heard after dark, many villagers fancied that the manner of slaying was exceedingly peculiar.

But the villagers did not discuss such things with the old man and his wife; because of the habitual expression on the withered faces of the two, and because their cottage was so small and so darkly hidden under spreading oaks and at the back of a neglected yard. In truth, much as the owners of cats hated these odd folk, they feared them more; and instead of berating them as brutal assassins, merely took care that no cherished pet or mouser should stray towards the remote hovel under the dark trees. When through some unavoidable oversight a cat was missed, and sounds were heard after dark, the loser would lament impotently; or console himself by thanking Fate that it was not one of his children who had thus vanished. For the people of Ulthar were simple, and knew not whence it is all cats first came.

One day a caravan of strange wanderers from the South entered the narrow cobbled streets of Ulthar. Dark wanderers they were, and unlike the other roving folk who passed through the village twice every year. In the market-place they told fortunes for silver, and bought gay beads from the merchants. What was the land of these wanderers none could tell; but it was seen that they were given to strange prayers and that they had painted on the sides of their wagons strange figures with human bodies and the heads of cats, hawks, rams and lions. And the leader of the caravan wore a head-dress with two horns and a curious disc between the horns.

There was in this singular caravan a little boy with no father or mother, but only a tiny black kitten to cherish. The plague had not been kind to him, yet had left him this small furry thing to mitigate his sorrow; and when one is very young, one can find great relief in the lively antics of a black kitten. So the boy whom the dark people called Menes smiled more often than he wept as he sat playing with his graceful kitten on the steps of an oddly painted wagon.

On the third morning of the wanderers' stay in Ulthar, Menes could not find his kitten; and as he sobbed aloud in the market-place certain villagers told him of the old man and his wife, and of sounds heard in the night. And when he heard these things his sobbing gave place to meditation, and finally prayer. He stretched out his arms towards the sun and prayed in a tongue no villager could understand; though indeed the villagers did not try very hard to understand, since their attention was mostly taken up by the sky and the odd shapes the clouds were assuming. It was very peculiar, but as the little boy uttered his petition there seemed to form overhead the shadowy, nebulous figures of exotic things; of hybrid creatures crowned with horn-flanked discs. Nature is full of such illusions to impress the imaginative.

That night the wanderers left Ulthar, and were never seen again. And the householders were troubled when they noticed that in all the village there was not a cat to be found. From each hearth the familiar cat had vanished; cats large and small, black, grey, striped, yellow and white. Old Kranon, the burgomaster, swore that the dark folks had taken the cats away in revenge for the killing of Menes' kitten; and cursed the caravan and the little boy. But Nith, the lean notary, declared that the old cotter and his wife were more likely persons to suspect; for their hatred of cats was notorious and increasingly bold.

Still, no one durst complain to the sinister couple; even when little Atal, the innkeeper's son, vowed that he had at twilight seen all the cats of Ulthar in that accursed yard under the trees, pacing very slowly and solemnly in a circle around the cottage, two abreast, as if in performance of some unheard-of rite of beasts. The villagers did know how much to believe from so small a boy; and though they feared that the evil pair had charmed the cats to their death, they preferred not to chide the old cotter till they met him outside his dark and repellent yard.

So Ulthar went to sleep in vain anger; and when the people awakened at dawn—behold! every cat was back at his accustomed hearth! Large and small, black, grey, striped, yellow and white, none was missing. Very sleek and fat did the cats appear, and sonorous with purring content. The citizens talked with one another of the affair, and marvelled not a little. Old Kranon again insisted that it was the dark folk who had taken them, since cats did not return alive from the cottage of the ancient man and his wife. But all agreed on one thing: that the refusal of the cats to eat their portions of meat or to drink their saucers of milk was exceedingly curious. And for two whole days the sleek, lazy cats of Ulthar would touch no food, but only doze by the fire or in the sun.

It was fully a week before the villagers noticed that no lights were appearing at dusk in the windows of the cottage under the trees. Then the lean Nith remarked that no one had seen the old man or his wife since the night the cats were away. In another week the burgomaster decided to overcome his fears and call at the strangely silent dwelling as a matter of duty, though in so doing he was careful to take with him Shang the blacksmith and Thul the cutter of stone as witnesses. And when they had broken down the frail door they found only this: two cleanly picked human skeletons on the earthen floor, and a number of singular beetles crawling in the shadowy corners.

There was subsequently much talk among the burgesses of Ulthar. Zath, the coroner, disputed at length with Nith, the lean notary; and Kranon and Shang and Thul were overwhelmed with questions. Even little Atal, the innkeeper's son, was closely questioned and given a sweetmeat as reward. They talked of the old cotter and his wife, of the caravan of dark wanderers, of small Menes and his black kitten, of the prayer of Menes and of the sky during that prayer, of the doings of the cats on the night the caravan left, and of what was later found in the cottage under the dark trees in the repellent yard.

And in the end the burgesses passed that remarkable law which is told of by traders in Hatheg and discussed by travellers in Nir; namely, that in Ulthar no man may kill a cat.

EYES OF THE PANTHER

by Ambrose Bierce

T HE DISTURBING IRONIE S *and nightmare themes of Ambrose Bierce's stories caused admirers to hail him as a successor to Poe. Bierce (1842–1914) also achieved notoriety as a bitterly satirical columnist for the press. Today he is perhaps best remembered for his short story of the American Civil War,* An Occurrence at Owl Creek Bridge, *which has been made into two distinguished films.*

Always unorthodox and rebellious in his behaviour, Bierce left behind a mystery as intriguing as anything he wrote. In 1913, at the age of seventy-one, he went off to Mexico to join Pancho Villa's cut-throat Revolutionaries—and was never seen again! From the scanty evidence it is generally assumed that he was murdered or executed the following year.

In The Devil's Dictionary, *a collection of his witty and cynical observations, Bierce defined the Cat as "a soft, indestructible automaton thoughtfully provided by nature to be kicked when things go wrong in the domestic circle".*

The feline of the following story is altogether more terrifying than that sorry beast.

I

ONE DOES NOT ALWAYS MARRY WHEN INSANE

A man and a woman—nature had done the grouping—sat on a rustic seat, in the late afternoon. The man was middle-aged, slender, swarthy, with the expression of a poet and the complexion of a pirate—a man at whom one would look again. The woman was young, blonde, graceful, with something in her figure and movements suggesting the word "lithe". She was habited in a grey gown with odd brown markings in the texture. She may have been beautiful; one could not readily say, for her eyes denied attention to all else. They were grey-green, long and narrow, with an expression defying analysis. One could only know that they were disquieting. Cleopatra may have had such eyes.

The man and the woman talked.

"Yes," said the woman, "I love you, God knows! But marry you, no. I cannot, will not."

"Irene, you have said that many times, yet always have denied me a reason. I've a right to know, to understand, to feel and prove my fortitude if I have it. Give me a reason."

"For loving you?"

The woman was smiling through her tears and her pallor. That did not stir any sense of humour in the man.

"No; there is no reason for that. A reason for not marrying me. I've a right to know. I must know. I will know!"

He had risen and was standing before her with clenched hands, on his face a frown—it might have been called a scowl. He looked as if he might attempt to learn by strangling her. She smiled no more—merely sat looking up into his face with a fixed, set regard that was utterly without emotion or sentiment. Yet it had something in it that tamed his resentment and made him shiver.

"You are determined to have my reason?" she asked in a tone that was entirely mechanical—a tone that might have been her look made audible.

"If you please—if I'm not asking too much."

Apparently this lord of creation was yielding some part of his dominion over his co-creature.

"Very well, you shall know: I am insane."

The man started, then looked incredulous and was conscious that he ought to be amused. But, again, the sense of humour failed him in his need and despite his disbelief he was profoundly disturbed by that which he did not believe. Between our convictions and our feelings there is no good understanding.

"That is what the physicians would say," the woman continued—
"if they knew. I might myself prefer to call it a case of 'possession'.
Sit down and hear what I have to say."

The man silently resumed his seat beside her on the rustic bench
by the wayside. Over-against them on the eastern side of the
valley the hills were already sunset-flushed and the stillness all about
was of that peculiar quality that foretells the twilight. Something
of its mysterious and significant solemnity had imparted itself to the
man's mood. In the spiritual, as in the material world, are signs and
presages of night. Rarely meeting her look, and whenever he did so
conscious of the indefinable dread with which, despite their feline
beauty, her eyes always affected him, Jenner Brading listened in
silence to the story told by Irene Marlowe. In deference to the
reader's possible prejudice against the artless method of an un-
practised historian the author ventures to substitute his own version
for hers.

II

A ROOM MAY BE TOO NARROW FOR THREE,
THOUGH ONE IS OUTSIDE

In a little log house containing a single room sparely and rudely
furnished, crouching on the floor against one of the walls, was a
woman, clasping to her breast a child. Outside, a dense unbroken
forest extended for many miles in every direction. This was at night
and the room was black dark: no human eye could have discerned
the woman and the child. Yet they were observed, narrowly, vigi-
lantly, with never even a momentary slackening of attention; and
that is the pivotal fact upon which this narrative turns.

Charles Marlowe was of the class, now extinct in this country,
of woodmen pioneers—men who found their most acceptable surroundings in sylvan solitudes that stretched along the eastern slope
of the Mississippi Valley, from the Great Lakes to the Gulf of
Mexico. For more than a hundred years these men pushed ever
westward, generation after generation, with rifle and axe, reclaim-

ing from Nature and her savage children here and there an isolated acreage for the plough, no sooner reclaimed than surrendered to their less venturesome but more thrifty successors. At last they burst through the edge of the forest into the open country and vanished as if they had fallen over a cliff. The woodman pioneer is no more; the pioneer of the plains—he whose easy task it was to subdue for occupancy two-thirds of the country in a single generation—is another and inferior creation. With Charles Marlowe in the wilderness, sharing the dangers, hardships and privations of that strange, unprofitable life, were his wife and child, to whom, in the manner of his class, in which the domestic virtues were a religion, he was passionately attached. The woman was still young enough to be comely, new enough to the awful isolation of her lot to be cheerful. By withholding the large capacity for happiness which the simple satisfactions of the forest life could not have filled, Heaven had dealt honourably with her. In her light household tasks, her child, her husband and her few foolish books, she found abundant provision for her needs.

One morning in midsummer Marlowe took down his rifle from the wooden hooks on the wall and signified his intention of getting game.

"We've meat enough," said the wife; "please don't go out today. I dreamed last night, O, such a dreadful thing! I cannot recollect it, but I'm almost sure that it will come to pass if you go out."

It is painful to confess that Marlowe received this solemn statement with less of gravity than was due to the mysterious nature of the calamity foreshadowed. In truth, he laughed.

"Try to remember," he said. "Maybe you dreamed that Baby had lost the power of speech."

The conjecture was obviously suggested by the fact that Baby, clinging to the fringe of his hunting-coat with all her ten pudgy thumbs, was at that moment uttering her sense of the situation in a series of exultant goo-goos inspired by sight of her father's raccoon-skin cap.

The woman yielded: lacking the gift of humour she could not hold out against his kindly badinage. So, with a kiss for the mother and a kiss for the child, he left the house and closed the door upon his happiness forever.

At nightfall he had not returned. The woman prepared supper and waited. Then she put Baby to bed and sang softly to her until she slept. By this time the fire on the hearth, at which she had cooked supper, had burned out and the room was lighted by a single candle. This she afterwards placed in the open window as a sign and welcome to the hunter if he should approach from that side. She had thoughtfully closed and barred the door against such wild animals as might prefer it to an open window—of the habits of beasts of prey in entering a house uninvited she was not advised, though with true female prevision she may have considered the possibility of their entrance by way of the chimney. As the night wore on she became not less anxious, but more drowsy, and at last rested her arms upon the bed by the child and her head upon the arms. The candle in the window burned down to the socket, sputtered and flared a moment and went out unobserved; for the woman slept and dreamed.

In her dreams she sat beside the cradle of a second child. The first one was dead. The father was dead. The home in the forest was lost and the dwelling in which she lived was unfamiliar. There were heavy oaken doors, always closed, and outside the windows, fastened into the thick stone walls, were iron bars, obviously (so she thought) a provision against Indians. All this she noted with an infinite self-pity, but without surprise—an emotion unknown in dreams. The child in the cradle was invisible under its coverlet which something impelled her to remove. She did so, disclosing the face of a wild animal! In the shock of this dreadful revelation the dreamer awoke, trembling in the darkness of her cabin in the wood.

As a sense of her actual surroundings came slowly back to her she felt for the child that was not a dream, and assured herself by its breathing that all was well with it; nor could she forbear to pass a hand lightly across its face. Then, moved by some impulse for which she probably could not have accounted, she rose and took the sleeping babe in her arms, holding it close against her breast. The head of the child's cot was against the wall to which the woman now turned her back as she stood. Lifting her eyes she saw two bright objects starring the darkness with a reddish-green glow. She took them to be two coals on the hearth, but with her returning sense of direction came the disquieting consciousness that they were not in that quarter of the room, moreover were too high, being nearly at the level of the eyes—of her own eyes. For these were the eyes of a panther.

The beast was at the open window directly opposite and not five paces away. Nothing but those terrible eyes was visible, but in the dreadful tumult of her feelings as the situation disclosed itself to her understanding she somehow knew that the animal was standing on its hinder feet, supporting itself with its paws on the window-ledge. That signified a malign interest—not the mere gratification of an indolent curiosity. The consciousness of the attitude was an added horror, accentuating the menace of those awful eyes in whose steadfast fire her strength and courage were alike consumed. Under their silent questioning she shuddered and turned sick. Her knees failed her, and by degrees, instinctively striving to avoid a sudden movement that might bring the beast upon her, she sank to the floor, crouched against the wall and tried to shield the babe with her trembling body without withdrawing her gaze from the luminous orbs that were killing her. No thought of her husband came to her in her agony—no hope nor suggestion of rescue or escape. Her capacity for thought and feeling had narrowed to the dimensions of a single emotion—fear of the animal's spring, of the impact of its body, the buffeting of its great arms, the feel of its teeth in her throat, the mangling of her babe. Motionless now and in absolute silence, she awaited her doom, the moments growing to hours, to years, to ages; and still those devilish eyes maintained their watch.

Returning to his cabin late at night with a deer on his shoulders Charles Marlowe tried the door. It did not yield. He knocked; there was no answer. He laid down his deer and went round to the window. As he turned the angle of the building he fancied he heard a sound as of stealthy footfalls and a rustling in the undergrowth of the forest but they were too slight for certainty, even to his practised ear. Approaching the window, and to his surprise finding it open, he threw his leg over the sill and entered. All was darkness and silence. He groped his way to the fireplace, struck a match and lit a candle. Then he looked about. Cowering on the floor against a wall was his wife, clasping his child. As he sprang towards her she rose and broke into laughter, long, loud, and mechanical, devoid of gladness and devoid of sense—the laughter that is not out of keeping with the clanking of a chain. Hardly knowing what he did he extended his arms. She laid the babe in them. It was dead—pressed to death in its mother's embrace.

III

THE THEORY OF THE DEFENCE

That is what occurred during a night in a forest, but not all of it did Irene Marlowe relate to Jenner Brading; not all of it was known to her. When she had concluded the sun was below the horizon and the long summer twilight had begun to deepen in the hollows of the land. For some moments Brading was silent, expecting the narrative to be carried forward to some definite connection with the conversation introducing it; but the narrator was as silent as he, her face averted, her hands clasping and unclasping themselves as they lay in her lap, with a singular suggestion of an activity independent of her will.

"It is a sad, a terrible story," said Brading at last, "but I do not understand. You call Charles Marlowe father; that I know. That he is old before his time, broken by some great sorrow, I have seen, or thought I saw. But, pardon me, you said that you—that you—"

"That I am insane," said the girl, without a movement of head or body.

"But, Irene, you say—please, dear, do not look away from me—you say that the child was dead, not demented."

"Yes, that one—I am the second. I was born three months after that night, my mother being mercifully permitted to lay down her life in giving me mine."

Brading was again silent; he was a trifle dazed and could not at once think of the right thing to say. Her face was still turned away. In his embarrassment he reached impulsively towards the hands that lay closing and unclosing in her lap, but something—he could not have said what—restrained him. He then remembered, vaguely, that he had never altogether cared to take her hand.

"Is it likely," she resumed, "that a person born under such circumstances is like others—is what you call sane?"

Brading did not reply; he was preoccupied with a new thought that was taking shape in his mind—what a scientist would have called an hypothesis; a detective, a theory. It might throw an added light, albeit a lurid one, upon such doubt of her sanity as her own assertion had not dispelled.

The country was still new and, outside the villages, sparsely populated. The professional hunter was still a familiar figure, and among his trophies were heads and pelts of the larger kinds of game. Tales variously credible of nocturnal meetings with savage animals in lonely roads were sometimes current, passed through the customary stages of growth and decay, and were forgotten. A recent addition to these popular apocrypha, originating, apparently, by spontaneous generation in several households, was a panther which had frightened some of their members by looking in at windows by night. The yarn had caused its little ripple of excitement—had even attained to the distinction of a place in the local newspaper; but Brading had given it no attention. Its likeness to the story to which he had just listened now impressed him as perhaps more than accidental. Was it not possible that the one story had suggested the other—that finding congenial conditions in a morbid mind and a fertile fancy, it had grown to the tragic tale he had heard?

Brading recalled certain circumstances of the girl's history and disposition, of which, with love's incuriosity, he had hitherto been heedless—such as her solitary life with her father, at whose house no one, apparently, was an acceptable visitor and her strange fear of the night, by which those who knew her best accounted for her never being seen after dark. Surely in such a mind imagination once kindled might burn with a lawless flame, penetrating and enveloping the entire structure. That she was mad, though the conviction gave him the acutest pain, he could no longer doubt; she had only mistaken an effect of her mental disorder for its cause, bringing into imaginary relation with her own personality the vagaries of the local myth-makers. With some vague intention of testing his new "theory", and no very definite notion of how to set about it he said, gravely, but with hesitation:

"Irene, dear, tell me—I beg you will not take offence, but tell me—"

"I have told you," she interrupted, speaking with a passionate earnestness that he had not known her to show— "I have already told you that we cannot marry; is anything else worth saying?"

Before he could stop her she had sprung from her seat and without another word or look was gliding away among the trees towards her father's house. Brading had risen to detain her; he stood watching her in silence until she had vanished in the gloom. Suddenly he started as if he had been shot; his face took on an expression of amazement and alarm: in one of the black shadows into which she had disappeared he had caught a quick, brief glimpse of shining eyes! For an instant he was dazed and irresolute; then he dashed into the wood after her, shouting: "Irene, Irene, look out! The panther! The panther!"

In a moment he had passed through the fringe of forest into open ground and saw the girl's grey skirt vanishing into her father's door. No panther was visible.

IV

AN APPEAL TO THE CONSCIENCE OF GOD

Jenner Brading, attorney-at-law, lived in a cottage at the edge of the town. Directly behind the dwelling was the forest. Being a bachelor, and therefore, by the Draconian moral code of the time and place denied the services of the only species of domestic servant known thereabout, the "hired girl," he boarded at the village hotel, where also was his office. The woodside cottage was merely a lodging maintained—at no great cost, to be sure—as an evidence of prosperity and respectability. It would hardly do for one to whom the local newspaper had pointed with pride as "the foremost jurist of his time" to be "homeless," albeit he may sometimes have sus-

pected that the words "home" and "house" were not strictly synony-
mous. Indeed, his consciousness of the disparity and his will to
harmonize it were matters of logical inference, for it was generally
reported that soon after the cottage was built its owner had made
a futile venture in the direction of marriage—had, in truth, gone so
far as to be rejected by the beautiful but eccentric daughter of Old
Man Marlowe, the recluse. This was publicly believed because he
had told it himself and she had not—a reversal of the usual order
of things which could hardly fail to carry conviction.

Brading's bedroom was at the rear of the house, with a single
window facing the forest. One night he was awakened by a noise
at that window; he could hardly have said what it was like. With a
little thrill of the nerves he sat up in bed and laid hold of the
revolver which, with a forethought most commendable in one ad-
dicted to the habit of sleeping on the ground floor with an open
window, he had put under his pillow. The room was in absolute
darkness, but being unterrified he knew where to direct his eyes, and
there he held them, awaiting in silence what further might occur.
He could now dimly discern the aperture—a square of lighter black.
Presently there appeared at its lower edge two gleaming eyes that
burned with a malignant lustre inexpressibly terrible! Brading's
heart gave a great jump, then seemed to stand still. A chill passed
along his spine and through his hair; he felt the blood forsake his
cheeks. He could not have cried out—not to save his life; but being
a man of courage he would not, to save his life, have done so if he
had been able. Some trepidation his coward body might feel, but his
spirit was of sterner stuff. Slowly the shining eyes rose with a steady
motion that seemed an approach, and slowly rose Brading's right
hand, holding the pistol. He fired!

Blinded by the flash and stunned by the report, Brading nevertheless heard, or fancied that he heard, the wild, high scream of the
panther, so human in sound, so devilish in suggestion. Leaping from
the bed he hastily clothed himself and, pistol in hand, sprang from
the door, meeting two or three men who came running up from the
road. A brief explanation was followed by a cautious search of the
house. The grass was wet with dew; beneath the window it had
been trodden and partly levelled for a wide space, from which a

devious trail, visible in the light of a lantern, led away into the bushes. One of the men stumbled and fell upon his hands, which, as he rose and rubbed them together, were slippery. On examination they were seen to be red with blood.

An encounter, unarmed, with a wounded panther was not agreeable to their taste; all but Brading turned back. He, with lantern and pistol, pushed courageously forward into the wood. Passing through a difficult undergrowth he came into a small opening, and there his courage had its reward, for there he found the body of his victim. But it was no panther. What it was is told, even to this day, upon a weather-worn headstone in the village churchyard, and for many years was attested daily at the graveside by the bent figure and sorrow-seamed face of Old Man Marlowe, to whose soul, and to the soul of his strange, unhappy child, peace. Peace and reparation.

THE BLACK CAT

by William Wintle

THE DESERVED FAME *of Poe's* The Black Cat *has led to the following, similarly-titled story being completely over-looked by anthologists.*

William James Wintle, a writer of the late Victorian period, collected old British folk songs for publication and wrote effusive works on Christianity and such contemporary heroines as Florence Nightingale and the Queen herself. These patriotic outpourings are now almost completely forgotten and it is his stories of the weird and macabre that collectors avidly seek today. Like his other ventures into this genre, The Black Cat *was originally dreamt up to entertain young relatives in the firelight glow of long wintry evenings—no doubt precipitating many a sleepless night for his young charges.*

If there was one animal that Sydney disliked more than another it was a cat. Not that he was not fond of animals in a general way—for he had a distinct affection for an aged retriever that had formerly been his—but somehow a cat seemed to arouse all that was worst in him. It always appeared to him that if he had passed through some previous stage of existence, he must have been a mouse or a bird and thus have inherited—so to speak—an instinctive dread and hatred for the enemy of his earlier days.

The presence of a cat affected him in a very curious fashion. There was first of all a kind of repulsion. The idea of the eyes of the animal being fixed on him; the thought of listening for a soundless tread; and the imagined touch of the smooth fur; all this made him shudder and shrink back. But this feeling quickly gave place to a still stranger fascination. He felt drawn to the creature that he feared—much as a bird is supposed, but quite erroneously, to be charmed by a snake. He wanted to stroke the animal and to feel its head rubbing against his hand: and yet at the same time the idea of the animal doing so filled him with a dread passing description. It was something like that morbid state in which a person finds actual physical pleasure in inflicting pain on himself. And then there was sheer undisguised fear. Pretend as he might, Sydney was in deadly fear when a cat was in the room. He had tried and tried, time and again, to overcome it; but without success. He had argued from the well-known friendliness of the domestic cat; from its notorious timidity; and from its actual inability to do any very serious harm to a strong and active man. But it was all of no use. He was afraid of cats; and it was useless to deny it.

At the same time, Sydney was no enemy to cats. He was the last man in the world to hurt one. No matter how much his slumber might be disturbed by the vocal efforts of a love-sick marauder on the roof in the small hours of the morning, he would never think of hurling a missile at the offender. The sight of a half-starved cat left behind when its owner was away in the holiday season filled him with a pity near akin to pain. He was a generous subscriber to the Home for Lost Cats. In fact, his whole attitude was inconsistent and contradictory. But there was no escape from the truth—he disliked and feared cats.

Probably this obsession was to some extent fostered by the fact that Sydney was a man of leisure. With more urgent matters to occupy his thoughts, he might have outgrown these fancies with the advance of middle age. But the possession of ample means, an inherited dislike for any kind of work calling for energy, and two or three interesting hobbies which filled up his time in an easy and soothing fashion, left him free to indulge his fancies. And fancies, when indulged, are apt to become one's masters in the end; and so it proved with Sydney.

He was engaged in writing a book on some phase of Egyptian life in the olden days, which involved considerable study of the collections in the British Museum and elsewhere, as well as much search for rare books among the antiquarian bookshops. When not out on these pursuits, he occupied an old house which like most old and rambling places of its kind was the subject of various queer stories among the gossips of the neighbourhood. Some tragedy was supposed to have happened there at some date not defined, and in consequence something was supposed to haunt the place and to do something from time to time. Among local gossips there was much value in that nebulous term "something", for it covered a multitude of inaccurate recollections and of foggy traditions. Probably Sydney had never heard the reputation of his house, for he led a retired life and had little to do with his neighbours. But if the tales had reached his ears, he gave no sign; nor was he likely to do so. Apart from the cat obsession, he was a man of eminently balanced mind. He was about the last person to imagine things or to be influenced by any but proved facts.

The mystery which surrounded his untimely end came therefore as a great surprise to his friends: and the horror that hung over his later days was only brought to partial light by the discovery of a diary and other papers which have provided the material for this history. Much still remains obscure, and cannot now be cleared up; for the only man who could perhaps throw further light on it is no longer with us. So we have to be content with such fragmentary records as are available.

It appears that some months before the end, Sydney was at home reading in the garden, when his eyes happened to rest upon a small heap of earth that the gardener had left beside the path. There was nothing remarkable about this; but somehow the heap seemed to fascinate him. He resumed his reading; but the heap of earth was insistent in demanding his attention. He could not keep his thoughts off it, and it was hard to keep his eyes off it as well. Sydney was not the man to give way to mental dissipation of this kind, and he resolutely kept his eyes fixed on his book. But it was a struggle; and in the end he gave in. He looked again at the heap; and this time with some curiosity as to the cause of so absurd an attraction.

Apparently there was no cause; and he smiled at the absurdity of the thing. Then he started up suddenly, for he saw the reason of it. The heap of earth was exactly like a black cat! And the cat was crouching as if to spring at him. The resemblance was really absurd,

for there were a couple of yellow pebbles just where the eyes should
have been. For the moment, Sydney felt all the repulsion and fear
that the presence of an actual cat would have caused him. Then he
rose from his chair, and kicked the heap out of any resemblance to
his feline aversion. He sat down again and laughed at the absurdity
of the affair—and yet it somehow left a sense of disquiet and of
vague fear behind. He did not altogether like it.

It must have been about a fortnight later when he was inspecting
some Egyptian antiquities that had recently reached the hands of
a London dealer. Most of them were of the usual types and did not
interest him. But a few were better worth attention; and he sat
down to examine them carefully. He was specially attracted by
some ivory tablets, on which he thought he could faintly trace the
remains of handwriting. If so, this was a distinct find, for private
memoranda of this sort are very rare and should throw light on
some of the more intimate details of private life of the period, which
are not usually recorded on the monuments. Absorbed in this study,
a sense of undefined horror slowly grew upon him and he found
himself in a kind of day dream presenting many of the uncanny
qualities of nightmare. He thought himself stroking an immense
black cat which grew and grew until it assumed gigantic proportions. Its soft fur thickened around his hands and entwined itself
around his fingers like a mass of silky, living snakes; and his skin
tingled with multitudinous tiny bites from fangs which were
venomous; while the purring of the creature grew until it became a
very roar like that of a cataract and overwhelmed his senses. He
was mentally drowning in a sea of impending catastrophe, when,
by an expiring effort, he wrenched himself free from the obsession
and sprang up. Then he discovered that his hand had been
mechanically stroking a small unopened animal mummy, which
proved on closer examination to be that of a cat.

The next incident that he seems to have thought worth recording
happened a few nights later. He had retired to rest in his usual
health and slept soundly. But towards morning his slumbers were
disturbed by a dream that recalled the kind of nocturnal fear that
is common in childhood. Two distant stars began to grow in size
and brilliancy until he saw that they were advancing through space

towards him with incredible speed. In a few moments they must overwhelm him in a sea of fire and flame. Onwards they came, bulging and unfolding like great flaming flowers, growing more dazzling and blinding at every moment; and then, just as they were upon him, they suddenly turned into two enormous cat's eyes, flaming green and yellow. He sprang up in bed with a cry, and found himself at once wide awake. And there on the window-sill lay a great black cat, glowering at him with lambent yellow eyes. A moment later the cat disappeared.

But the mysterious thing of it was that the window-sill was not accessible to anything that had not wings. There was no means by which a cat could have climbed to it. Nor was there any sign of a cat in the garden below.

The date of the next thing that happened is not clear, for it does not appear to have been recorded at the time. But it would seem to have been within a few days of the curious dream. Sydney had occasion to go to a cupboard which was kept locked. It contained manuscripts and other papers of value; and the key never left his possession. To his knowledge the cupboard had not been opened for at least a month past. He now had occasion to refer to a collection of notes in connection with his favourite study. On opening the cupboard, he was at once struck by a curious odour. It was not exactly musky, but could only be described as an animal odour, slightly suggestive of that of a cat. But what at once arrested Sydney's notice and caused him extreme annoyance was the fact that the papers had been disturbed. The loose papers contained in some pigeon-holes at the back had been drawn forwards into a loose heap on the shelf. They looked for all the world like a nest, for they had been loosely arranged in a round heap with a depression in the middle. It looked as if some animal had coiled itself up to sleep there; and the size of the depression was just such as would be made by a cat.

Sydney was too much annoyed by the disturbance of his papers to be greatly impressed at the moment by their curious arrangement; but it came home to him as a shock when he began to gather the papers together and set them in order. Some of them seemed to be slightly soiled, and on closer examination he found that they were besprinkled with short black hairs like those of a cat.

About a week afterwards he returned later in the evening than usual, after attending a meeting of a scientific society to which he belonged. He was taking his latch key from his pocket to open the door when he thought that something rubbed against his leg. Looking down, he saw nothing; but immediately afterwards he felt it again, and this time he thought he saw a black shadow beside his right foot. On looking more closely, nothing was to be seen; but as he went into the house he distinctly felt something soft brush against his leg. As he paused in the hall to remove his overcoat, he saw a faint shadow which seemed to go up the stairs. It was certainly only a shadow and nothing solid, for the light was good and he saw it clearly. But there was nothing in motion to account for the passing shadow. And the way the shadow moved was curiously suggestive of a cat.

The next notes in the book that Sydney seems to have devoted to this curious subject appear to be a series of mere coincidences: and the fact that he thought them worth recording shows only too clearly to what an extent his mind was now obsessed. He had taken the numerical value of the letters C, A, T, in the alphabet, 3, 1, and 20 respectively, and by adding them together had arrived at the total 24. He then proceeded to note the many ways in which this number had played its part in the events of his life. He was born on the 24th of the month, at a house whose number was 24; and his mother was 24 years old at the time. He was 24 years old when his father died and left him the master of a considerable fortune. That was just 24 years ago. The last time he had balanced his affairs, he found that he was worth in invested funds—apart from land and houses—just about 24 thousand pounds. At three different periods, and in different towns, he had chanced to live at houses numbered 24; and that was also the number of his present abode. Moreover the number of his ticket for the British Museum Reading Room ended with 24, and both his doctor and his solicitor were housed under that same persistent number. Several more of these coincidences had been noted by him; but they were rather far-fetched and are not worth recording here. But the memoranda concluded with the ominous question, "Will it all end on the 24th?"

Soon after these notes were written, a much more serious affair had to be placed on record. Sydney was coming downstairs one evening, when he noticed in a badly lighted corner of the staircase something that he took to be a cat. He shrank back with his natural dislike for the animal; but on looking more closely he saw that it was nothing more than a shadow cast by some carving on the stair-head. He turned away with a laugh; but, as he turned, it certainly seemed that the shadow moved! As he went down the stairs he twice stumbled in trying to save himself from what he thought was a cat in danger of being trodden upon; and a moment later he seemed to tread on something soft that gave way and threw him down. He fell heavily and shook himself badly.

On picking himself up with the aid of his servant he limped into his library, and there found that his trousers were torn from a little above the ankle. But the curious thing was that there were three parallel vertical tears—just such as might be caused by the claws of a cat. A sharp smarting led to further investigation; and he then found that there were three deep scratches on the side of his leg, exactly corresponding with the tears in the trousers.

In the margin of the page on which he recorded this accident, he has added the words, "This cat means mischief." And the whole tone of the remaining entries and of the few letters that date from this time shows only too clearly that his mental outlook was more or less tinged and obscured by gloomy forebodings.

It would seem to have been on the following day that another disturbing trifle occurred. Sydney's leg still pained him, and he spent the day on a couch with one or two favourite books. Soon after two o'clock in the afternoon, he heard a soft thud, such as might be caused by a cat leaping down from a moderate height. He looked up, and there on the window-sill crouched a black cat with gleaming eyes; and a moment later it sprang into the room. But it never reached the floor—or, if it did, it must have passed through it! He saw it spring; he saw it for the moment in mid-air; he saw it about to alight on the floor; and then—it was not there!

He would have liked to believe that it was a mere optical delusion; but against that theory stood the awkward fact that the cat in springing down from the window knocked over a flower-pot; and there lay the broken pieces in evidence of the fact.

He was now seriously scared. It was bad enough to find himself seeing things that had no objective reality; but it was far worse to be faced by happenings that were certainly real, but not to be accounted for by the ordinary laws of nature. In this case the broken flower-pot showed that if the black cat was merely what we call a ghost for lack of any more convenient term, it was a ghost that was capable of producing physical effects. If it could knock a flower-pot over, it could presumably scratch and bite—and the prospect of being attacked by a cat from some other plane of existence will hardly bear being thought of.

Certainly it seemed that Sydney had now real ground for alarm. The spectre cat—or whatever one likes to call it—was in some way gaining power and was now able to manifest its presence and hostility in more open and practical fashion. That same night saw a proof of this. Sydney dreamed that he was visiting the Zoological Gardens when a black leopard of ferocious aspect escaped from its cage and sprang upon him. He was thrown backwards to the ground and pinned down by the heavy animal. He was half crushed by its weight; its claws were at his throat; its fierce yellow eyes were staring into his face; when the horror of the thing brought the dream to a sudden end and he awoke. As consciousness returned he was aware of an actual weight on his chest; and on opening his eyes he looked straight into the depths of two lambent yellow flames set in a face of velvet black. The cat sprang off the bed and leaped through the window. But the window was closed and there was no sound of breaking glass.

Sydney did not sleep much more that night. But a further shock awaited him on rising. He found some small blood stains on his pillow; and an inspection before the looking glass showed the presence of two groups of tiny wounds on his neck. They were little more than pin-pricks; but they were arranged in two semi-circular groups, one on either side of the neck and just such as might be caused by a cat trying to grasp the neck between its two forepaws.

This was the last incident recorded in Sydney's diary; and the serious view that he took of the situation is shown by certain letters that he wrote during the day, giving final instructions to his executors and settling various details of business—evidently in view of his approaching end.

What happened in the course of the final scene of the tragedy we can only guess from the traces left behind: but there is sufficient evidence to show that the horror was an appalling one.

The housekeeper seems to have been awakened once during the night by a strange noise which she could only describe as being like an angry cat snarling; while the parlour maid, whose room was immediately above that occupied by Sydney, says that she dreamt that she heard her master scream horribly once or twice.

In the morning, Sydney did not answer when called at his usual hour; and, as the door was found to be locked, the housekeeper presently procured assistance and had it broken open. He was found crouching on the floor and leaning against the wall opposite the window. The carpet was saturated with blood; and the cause was quickly evident. The unfortunate man's throat had been torn open on either side, both jugular veins being severed. So far as could be made out, he had retired to bed and had been attacked during sleep, for the sheets were bespattered with blood. He had apparently got out of bed in his struggles to overcome the Thing that had him fast in its fearful grip. The look of horror on his distorted face was said by the witnesses to be past description.

Both window and door were fastened, and there was nothing to show how the assailant entered. But there was something to show how it left. The bloodstains on the floor recorded the footprints of a gigantic cat. They led across the floor from the corpse to the opposite wall—and there they ceased. The cat never came back; but whether it passed through the solid wall or melted into thin air, no one knows. In some mysterious way it came and went; and in passing it did this deed of horror.

It was a curious coincidence that the tragedy took place on Christmas Eve—the 24th day of the month!

THE CHILD WATCHER

by Ernest Harrison

THE REVEREND ERNEST HARRISON *is the author of four theological works, several radio and television plays and numerous short tales of mystery. Born and educated in England, he now lives in Toronto, Canada, where he is Dean of Arts at a Polytechnical Institute.*

This brief but shattering story plays with the reader as a Cat with a mouse—then leaps in, mercilessly, for the kill. It's a story you will want to read again. Often.

Esther looked down at the baby with interest. He lay in his crib, playing solemnly with his toes, his bright eyes intent on the one that stuck out at such an odd angle. Suddenly he tired of his researches, and turning over on his stomach tried to edge himself to the corner of his crib.

Though unable to smile, Esther felt a warm glow within her as a movement in her womb held out its promise of fulfilment. A flood of confused memories swept over her—the moment of ecstasy, the vague sadness which followed, and now the nearness of birth. These things could not be put into words, perhaps not even into thoughts, but the emotions ran strong in her. She looked down once more at the baby. Soon, the movement in her belly told her, soon she— Her thoughts broke off in a blurred image she could not quite capture.

The baby made an awkward turn, and his nappy pin opened. A sharp prick, and he was howling. The door opened within seconds, and the anxious mother swept into the room.

"My baby, my precious little boy . . . Diddums cry for mummy?" She picked him up in her arms and snuggled him to her breast.

"Look, Esther, isn't he a *silly* little boy to cry for his mummy like that, when Esther is here?" A piercing howl as her hand pressed the pin into his skin again, and she discovered the cause of his complaint. All was contrition. "Oh, so that's it! Did *nasty* mummy hurt her little darling? There, there . . ." The words ran on without end.

Esther felt slightly sick.

Her first pains soon came, and then the joy of birth. It is easy to be cynical about the possessiveness of mother love, but nature imposes it at the very moment that a life comes into the world. And by the same token, once the first sound of a new breathing comes, there is bitterness if the life is snatched away . . .

It was later, and Esther once more looked down at the baby, but now there was envy in her heart. His mother had patted and cuddled him, unaware of Esther's turmoil. Now she had gone from the room, and Esther remained to watch the child.

She gulped slightly. The memories of ecstasy had faded. Vague thoughts tumbled through her mind. She recalled the pains vividly, and the cries of life. Then the joy, so abruptly ended. She did not understand death, or what distinguished it from life and left blackness in the heart. If the mother who had just left the room had thought of asking her, Esther would have remained dumb.

But she knew what hate was, and envy. The baby began to crow with pleasure. "Come," his look declared, "don't be sad, Esther. I don't know what makes you so unhappy, but the world isn't worth it. You'll forget, all right, just as I do. See, I've got a great big foot to show you . . . I know how mad mummy always makes you. She makes me mad, too. Sometimes, that is. Come *on*, Esther, snap out of it. Anyway, I love you, don't I? Now, doesn't that make it up to you?"

Esther looked at him without expression, and he turned away to explore the pillow.

Without warning the hate in her heart overflowed. She knew suddenly what she wanted to do. She turned her head towards the door, listening carefully. There was no sound.

She turned back to the baby, watched his antics. She was still not certain how she would do it—only that she wanted to do it more than anything in the world.

The child's bottom stuck in the air, moving from side to side as he tried to push his head through the rails of his crib.

Esther passed the tip of her tongue through her lips, feeling a slight constriction at the throat. She moved forward, then stopped. The baby, finding his head was too large, pulled back, wriggled over on to his back.

He was about to put his feet up, touch them with his hands, when his eye caught Esther's expression. He raised his voice—a sudden, choking scream; and Esther fell upon him. The cry rose to a shriek. Pulsing with her whole hatred of the world, Esther tore madly at him.

The door banged open and the baby's mother rushed into the room. Esther whirled, at bay. But then she was struggling for her own life, being choked out of her by the woman who had drowned her newborn kittens.

NOTES

Beware the Cat
The ingredients of the magic cake are enough, one would think,
to turn *Macbeth's* witches green! They include the heart, kidney
and liver of a cat; the heart and lights of a fox; a hare's brain and
a hedgehog's kidney.

The Vampire Cat
In July 1929 the *Sunday Express* reported that the Vampire Cat of
Nabéshima was once more about its nightly business, terrorising the
beautiful wives of the descendants of the Samurai warriors.

The White Cat
The *Journal for the Society for Psychical Research* for January
1927 told of a ghostly white kitten that made many appearances
over a period of thirteen years, often being seen by several witnesses
at a time. And "every such appearance of the white kitten was

shortly followed either by the death of a person related or the beginning of a fatal disease".

There are also many instances of *black* phantom Cats whose
banshee-like appearances are followed by a death in the house.
Occult experts are in agreement that of animal ghosts, those of
Cats are by far the most active.

Ancient Sorceries

When he conceived this story, Blackwood probably had in mind the
Basque region of France which was notorious in the sixteenth and
seventeenth centuries for the outrageous behaviour of its witches
who were particularly adept at changing into Cats. Writing in
1612, the Witch-hunter Pierre de Lancre, who was responsible for
sending many alleged witches to the stake, estimated that as many
as 100,000 witches attended the great Sabbats in this region. Even
today, in this part of France where the natives have their own
language and culture and the racial origins of the people are obscure,
there is a strong belief in witchcraft and lycanthropy.

"Witches still appear in the shape of cats, generally black ones.
About two years ago, we were told of a man, who, at midnight,
chopped off the ear of a black cat who was bewitching his cattle,
and lo! in the morning it was a woman's ear, with an ear-ring still
in it."

From *Basque Legends* by the Reverend Wentworth Webster, 1877.

The Cats of Ulthar

Amongst Lovecraft's papers was found this note which is believed
to have been the basis for his writing *The Cats of Ulthar*: "The
cat is the soul of antique Aegyptus and bearer of tales from forgotten (empires of) cities in Meroe and Ophir. He is the kin of the
jungle's lords, and heir to the secrets of hoary and sinister Africa.
The Sphinx is his cousin, and he speaks her language; but is more
ancient than the Sphinx, and remembers that which she hath forgotten."

The premise of Lovecraft's tale is far from fictional for in many
parts of ancient Egypt the cat was sacred and to kill one was con-

sidered an unforgiveable blasphemy. The Greek historian Herodotus, who passed through Egypt in about 450 B.C. and visited the temple of the Cat-goddess Bastet at Bubastis, tells of an ignorant Roman legionary who struck a cat and was immediately killed by a mob of furious bystanders. Perhaps fear of retribution from some non-human source overcame their fear of the Romans.

The Cats of Ulthar make an appearance in one of Lovecraft's longer stories, *The Dream Quest of Unknown Kadath*, where they play an almost heroic part, rescuing the story's hero, Randolph Carter, from a nameless fate at the hands (?) of some "Toad-things". In this story, which is lighter and more whimsical in mood than most of his work, Lovecraft describes how the cats use city roof-tops as springboards to the dark side of the Moon which is reserved for their play and recreation.

The Eyes of the Panther
There are innumerable examples in the records of witch-trials in Europe and America of witches masquerading as some form of feline in order to work their mischief. Usually the deception is uncovered when a paw or other part of the cat is lopped off by a sword-stroke and, later, a human being is discovered to have a corresponding limb missing.

Scottish witches were particularly fond of assuming the guise of cats and in 1596 some impudent witches in feline shape were seen to dance merrily round the Fish Cross in Aberdeen. Isobel Grierson was strangled and burnt at Edinburgh for bewitching Adam Clark: "in likeness of her own cat, accompanied with a great number of other cats, in a devilish manner, entered within their house, where they made a great and tearful noise and trouble; whereby the said Adam, then lying in bed with his wife and servants that were then in the house apprehended such a great fear that they were likely to go mad".

Another Scottish witch, Isobel Gowdie, revealed the following spell for regaining human form when in the shape of a cat. It has to be repeated three times:

Catt, catt, God send thee a blak shott
I am in a cattis liknes just now,
Bot I sal be in a womanis liknes
    ewin now.
Catt, catt, God send thee a blak shott.